Large Format Paper Edition
Continuous Printing
First Published January 24, 2014
Issue "C", January 9, 2025

Published congruently with
Limited Hand-Bound Print Edition
version r-104

Library of Congress
Control Number: 2011922059

ISBN: 9780983857532

Published by
WEST WINTER PRESS
Sky Valley, California, USA

eyes full
of light
and laughter

love stories by

JOHN CAEDAN

the stories

From the Author

This is a book of intimacies.
Twenty-six love stories.

You will find things missing ... cheating,
boredom, cruelty, cold beds, jaded aspect ... can
this book be believed? In a hard age, is love
sublime – or a delusion?

We still say, "I am in love with you."

A love may grow – or go. Either way, we crave
it, seek it, and laugh in amazement when struck
by lightning.

John Caedan
Front Range, Rocky Mountains
Spring, 2014

Format note: the style of ragged-right line was
deliberately chosen. It allows each word and
letter to rest in its proper bed. This was deemed
suitable for prose walking with poetry.

as annoying as ice cream

J ust before going too far, her hand froze. She
stood naked, a little wet from the shower,
considering. Then, instead of a big blast from
the atomizer, she spritzed a faint smudge of
mist into the air, and with eyes closed stepped
into the fragrant cloud with a graceful twist and
glide. The exotically scented fog settled on her
hair, shoulders, and breasts. She held still, rapt in
the thrill of it, the sophisticated scent so delicate it
could afford to be this sweet, certain never to cloy
the senses.

Breaking the spell, she padded to the side of the
bed. With sure hand she bypassed two lesser
options and lifted a white camisole top, holding it
in place, consulting the mirror for confirmation.
Yes, just so. She pulled on black underwear
bottoms and stylish trousers with a slender belt
first, then socks.

Confidence was high.

One quandary remained, however. Cotton top
in hand, she stood in the center of the room,
bottom lip caught between teeth, breathing
slowly. Female acuity raced in consideration of
much. Momentarily, she took a step across the
room, opened her best underwear drawer, and

selected the needed garment.

Inevitably, ice cream made an appearance in the early afternoon. With ironic teasing running strong, the ice cream ritual did not raise embarrassment, nor had the carousel of wooden horses, nor the Ferris wheel – not even the preposterously romantic rowboat ride.

"Chocolate?" he asked.

"Of course. Is there any other flavor? You too, right?"

He shook his head with mock gravity and ordered vanilla. They strolled out onto a grassy area between two old-fashioned amusements, letting the sun into their faces as they licked down the creamy cones, glancing in each other's eyes often, teasing the date-cute.

"We deserve some sort of award, don't you think?" he asked.

"Why?"

"For bearing up under such a clichéd date without cracking."

She laughed. "Who do you think is winning?"

"I am. I'm the man. This date is something no man should ever put up with."

"But there's pressure on the woman, too, don't forget. What if I'm being too suffocating? That's death, right?"

"Yep, suffocating is fatal." He sobered. "But, nope. Not."

Serious ice cream business quieted them. They traded tastes. She stopped their walk and turned to face him.

"It goes both ways," she said.

He agreed with a nod.

She grew impish. "Do you think we're in the blind spot?"

"The what?"

"The blind spot. That's when everything that would normally be annoying doesn't even bother you a bit. You are trying ... the two people are trying to please each other, to get to ... to get to mating, and so nature pushes everything aside except what makes them feel good about each other." The heat of daring shone on her face.

He stared at her, frozen.

"I saw it on the Discovery Channel," she threw in.

A smile broke across his features. "You're about as annoying as ice cream."

During the afternoon the irony vanished – they rode no more fairground rides, engaging with heads close together on a bench at the edge of the lake instead, exposing privacies, offering opportunities for trusting. Not shallow, either of them, they tangled splendidly, finding themselves across the boundary of risk. She noticed how excited she was underneath, yet how detached from expectation, a quite curious confluence, as if watching someone other than her falling for him.

Near sunset they headed to the parking lot in a comfortable silence. He broke it out of the blue.

"I know how we can find out," he said.

"Find out what?"

"If we're in the blind spot."

"Oh, that! How?"

"Well, on a date like this ... the kiss at the end ... you know ..."

"The kiss?"

"Yes. Can't you feel it coming?"

"I felt it coming, all right. You should have kissed me an hour ago. On the Ferris wheel."

"We'll find out in the kiss."

They stared at each other, realization dawning, eyes growing big. "It's In His Kiss!" they shouted together. This made them silly, made them sing lines of the famous song, playing with each other's delightedness on a fine edge. "If you want to know ..."

He took her by the wrist, drew her behind a tree at the fringe of the parking lot, jolted to a stop and spun her body into his. She fell inside, head tilting to take his mouth, pressing with hands at the back of his head to show willingness. His arms around her waist cinched tight.

The sweet kiss held fresh for long seconds. His lips were never stiff or cold, never. Little pleasure sounds he could not contain thrilled like tiny leaps of joy. The scent of his skin imprinted on her, forever to hold the power of this moment in it.

As if summoned by gods, a force gathered in her pelvis and pooled at the base of her spine. It waited.

In a flashing instant, she gave her will. A whimper escaped her throat. The energy exploded up her back, down her arms, into the fingertips tangled in his hair. She arched against him, raising her breasts, turning from side to side to settle them deeply, offering their loveliness.

Shuddering, he took her tighter in embrace. She melted in.

Then the kiss blossomed anew – it began at the touch of their lips, unfolded high, then reached back beyond the mind's eye to approach the open heart.

She lifted her mouth from his to find his eyes searching her, holding her, adoring her. Her gaze fell to his mouth, which had made hers burn.

"Less annoying than ice cream," he said.

"Yes," she whispered.

As they made their way to the car, slowly because of the difficulty of taking their eyes from each other, she grew aware of a heartbreaking sweet scent, like a cloud of joy around her head. She put her fingers at the top edge of her camisole and pulled it open slightly. The scent increased. She realized it was the last of the incredible perfume from this morning, boiled by love.

john caedan

her good helping magic

S asha waited on him today.
 Both she and Marianne noted his arrival, the fine-looking college type entering the store for the tenth time in ten days. Sasha stepped forward.

"Well, hi."

"Here I am again. You know, right? Same thing, same flowers, same color."

Sasha slipped into the walk-in through glass doors. They had stocked up, knowing he would be coming in every day – until he did not. In the corner stood a bucket of long-stemmed yellow roses, fresh, vibrant, tightly closed. She counted out a dozen.

"Any card today, sir?" she asked, passing him on the way to the wrapping area.

"No, not necessary," he said with thin courage. "After all, the flowers say all there is to say."

Sasha and Marianne laughed. Sasha deftly constructed a stylish bouquet by surrounding the roses with baby's-breath and green leatherleaf, whispering their Latin names to herself in a low whisper, as was her way – *gypsophila elegans* and *chamaedaphne calyculata.*

The cash transaction duly performed, she handed over the beautiful package with care, loving the blooms before they departed on their mission. She looked up at her customer, expecting the usual curt thank-you. Instead, he paused, looking glum.

"How much does that make it?"

Sasha did a quick mental calculation. "About two hundred and twenty-eight dollars so far. You caught us on a sale day twice."

The young man nodded, turned, and exited the store, troubled head held high.

Sasha walked over to her friend.

"I'm worrying worse now," she said. "He must have done something really really really bad."

"I think it's something else," said Marianne. "He fell in love too fast. She's tempted, but she hasn't even kissed him yet."

Either way, Sasha sent an ounce of her good helping magic down the street to follow him home.

then it melted me

"I need a word that rhymes with 'cheat'."

"Bleat," he said immediately.

"Bleat sweet neat wheat, it's an easy word to rhyme, but bleat is cool," she said with that faraway look a writer gets when here ... but not here.

"Do I get a credit?"

"A credit on a gift card? I don't think so, mister."

"The gift is from both of us."

She declined to contest the point, but he didn't count it a victory. Her focus fell to the cream-colored paper pad in her left hand. In her face appeared that familiar set of the mouth and glint in the eye as she wrote a line or two – the brilliant lamp was lit.

This was their fine cold Saturday morning, sprawled across a favorite sofa, jumbled together, jeans to jeans, sweater to sweater. She lay back against his encircling left arm with legs draped over his hips. This setup afforded delicious proximity to her shoulder and neck and made the tangling of hair inevitable.

"Cheat and bleat sounds dirty."

"Shh."

"It's a wedding, should we be dirty-joking?"

"Shush or else," she spat out, and continued jotting.

He decided to hold back his meddling, not so simple considering the zing of their teasing recently. He credited prior restraint in these situations for the fact she even deigned to write 'word one' while this close. Then, this was not the serious stuff – it was one of her famous limericks.

He stayed well clear anytime it was serious. Navigating their space when her intensity reached escape velocity could be perilous. Often, she would not actually have pen to paper for hours yet be fully in the throes. Then he needed utmost sensitivity and detachment – the woman aflame, but you cannot touch. Delicious aggravation. Just now, however, her modality added to the fun – she was off.

So, hurry up with the damn gift card, he wanted to say. It was oh so difficult to not move his right hand, resting precariously at her waistline.

"Wait, wait ..." she said. Her pen moved furiously. "Got it, nailed it."

"Finally. Are we going to get kicked out of the reception?"

"You mean when I read it?"

"Yeah, like that time you wrote one for Serge when he left for Harvard Divinity School, remember, at his party?"

"Oh yeah, the one with the juicy parts of the

Song of Solomon in it."

"He got mad."

"I know, but you know what, he forgave me later," she said. "It's in the damn Bible."

"Or that time at your sister's shower, how filthy was that?"

"Never mind that one, those girls were bawdy. They were howling."

"So?"

"Okay, okay." She read it theatrically ...

> *"Now here's to a guy who won't cheat;*
> *For his dream-girl he's always in heat.*
> *She's likewise as strong*
> *in a dress or a thong,*
> *So to dance at their wedding is sweet."*

Stunning. Ridiculous. Brilliant.

"Dirty and sentimental at the same time."

"That's right." Her face shone with mischief and the flared nostrils of smart jesting.

Now! Quick! Her shoulder, her neck, her mouth. Yes, to get her worked up from lurid pertinacious kissing.

"Oh great, you're in heat!"

"I'm in love," he said, dripping with irony. He kissed wetter.

"Really."

"Let's get married."

"What, again?"

"I want to hear you say those vows again. Then I want to consummate. More than once."

"Oh my God, what did I vow? I can't

remember."

"You promised to obey."

"Sorry, that can't be right."

"That's what every woman has to promise."

"In your twisted dreams."

"That's what Andi is going to promise Jake this afternoon."

"No." Suddenly, she was dead serious. Ribald-girl had slammed on the brakes – such was his mercurial mate.

"No?"

She untangled herself and bounced up from the sofa. He would not say their fun was ruined, exactly, but she clearly had something up. He knew she wanted a scotch. Three years quit, but he could feel her reaching for one. She walked over to the bay window and looked out on the cold morning.

"Andi told me what their vows are going to be."

"Uh-oh."

"No, there's nothing really wrong with them. But here we go again, two great people, and do they know what the hell they're getting into?"

"Did we?" he asked quietly.

"She said they went around and around, even got into a fight about it about a month ago, but then they figured it out, said they couldn't improve on the standard."

"Wow."

"They are both going to say the same thing to each other, 'I promise to love, honor, and cherish until death us do part'."

"Wow."

"Don't you think it's perfectly right? And perfectly wrong?"

"Are you sure you want to talk about this now?"

"Yes," she said. "Something got me when I was writing that silly thing. I felt it ping me."

He walked over to her. The natural light from outside filled her face. He was grateful she was only determined, not down.

"Last spring," she said.

"Oh."

"I never really explained what happened."

"I thought what happened is, we started all over again," he said. Carefully.

"Let me tell you one more thing, okay? It's important."

"Okay."

"To this day, I don't really know what set it off, but it was a dead zone. That's all it was, only that, a dead zone."

A rush of blood raced through him. He had never asked to look under this rock. Instead, a full-out campaign to get back under her skin. His result – the last eight months of renewed joy. That had answered all. Which way would the rock tumble now?

"Did you fall out of love with me?"

She looked in his eyes with open soul. "Yes."

He didn't look away. He nodded.

Then, "No," she whispered.

"You didn't?"

"I fell out of loving."

A look of pain came over her, old pain that possessed no purchase now.

"It's the wrong vow. You can't promise you'll always love," she said.

"No."

"It's too big. You can't control it all the time."

"No, you can't."

"Instead, you have to vow to do what you did. For months. To re-woo."

"What?"

"You fought to get me back. You didn't stop believing in us. You knew it was gone, but you came after me."

"That Loving Feeling. Was gone from your eyes," he said. Not to mention the tenderness gone from her fingertips.

"Yes. You even tried to write me a poem once, remember?"

He groaned. "Oh, please. Please tell me you burned it."

A rueful smile and a shake of her head. "I have it."

"I thought the night I washed your hair and gave that massage, I think that helped."

"I started out hating that. Please don't be hurt, but your touch that night first revolted me. But then it melted me." She looked out the window with a small smile. "It was only a dead zone."

She took a step forward and tilted her face to him. Her gaze held his, steady. In an instant of time he saw everything come to a point in her eyes.

"I was true," she said.

"I don't want to know."

"Yes, you do. There was a moment. I didn't cheat."

A terror of devastation and rage not suffered came flying into the room. It wanted revenge. He opened a door and kicked it out, as a man does.

"Since the day we met? Even when you were in Portland during the dead zone and not calling me and I was here for nearly three weeks suffering? You were alone in bed?"

"Yes," she said. "Since the day we met, you are my only."

He took her in his arms. She encircled him with hers. It was consummation. He stood on the rock with everything possessed, to have and to hold.

only dreamed you said it

She rolled out of the bathroom in full momentum of Monday rush. No intention to wake him ... she stopped short ... he was not in the bed.

She found him blocking the front door like Valentine's bodyguard.

"Not so fast," he said.

"I've got a meeting."

"I only need thirty seconds."

"Oh, man ..."

"Thirty good ones."

She cooled her outward-bound drives, lowered her eyes to put on the soft girl, shook her head with a sigh, and raised her face to him.

"There's always one second that haunts you good from the night before," he said. "You can't stop thinking about. It wells up."

"Again? You always bring this up ..."

"Give me yours."

"You have to give one too."

"Don't worry."

She blinked. She found it on the next inhale. "It was right before I fell asleep. I thought I heard you say, 'you'll find something spectacular on your desk at work tomorrow.' Right? Did you whisper that?"

"Yes."

"That was cruel. It haunted me all night, even when I thought I only dreamed you said it. What is it?"

"The essence of us."

"Oh, for crying out loud."

"Calm down."

"Okay, okay, okay ... what's yours?"

"Right before dinner, we were kissing. You pulled away to go get the wine. But you stopped, turned around, put your hand on your heart, and sent everything to me across the kitchen."

"Oh."

"I fell in love with you for the four-hundredth time," he said.

She blushed. First time since high school.

"Good thing," she said. "That brings you even with me."

Rushing, she did not fully close the door to her office behind. Ten minutes later something odious wafted in – two girl interns, only a few years younger than she, in the corridor talking Monday morning trash, bragging about their dirty weekend, cruel tricks to humiliate boys after hook-up sex, sloppy drunk, flipped wild on Vitamin-X.

She stepped around her desk and swept the door to her office shut with a bang. Laughter burst from the two girls, and snarking giggles.

It took a minute of steady breathing with eyes closed to retrieve full equanimity.

Work-focus bubbled up. Just before she engaged, her eyes came to rest on the corner of her desk. She reached over and fetched the small crystal bud vase, temporarily setting it in front of her keyboard – three stalks, each only four inches long, with precious white blossoms shaped like tiny bells. With surprising potency for their size, they perfumed the office with sweetness and innocence. She let the scent inflame, thrilled that so small a bud could open the heart.

"That's four hundred and one," she whispered.

john caedan

basking in the young sun

Gabrielle's grandmother died in the spring, a week after the girl's seventeenth birthday. Happily, they had spent three vibrant days together at Grandmama's flat in Montreal after the birthday party, a blessing of adieu.

Back in Boston, Gabrielle received the news on a day early in May. At first, the fact that Grandmama died quietly in her sleep was a comfort, yet because this wonderful lady was loved in so many places of strength in the young girl's heart, pain would emerge at intervals for years.

Due to her fine character, Gabrielle never dulled the loss with forgetfulness or diminishment, but rather revivified their times together, speaking to her quietly in French, as if a fine response, elegant, wise, delightful, were to be expected on the next breath. Grandmama remained alive to her in this way.

Nine years later. Journal entry for June 23

So much happiness, yet with tears as well in the eyes of many I love. Little Angela cried three times, I believe. I know them to be tears of joy for me, and I beheld the radiance in her face. Tomorrow, perhaps, I

will write down one or two heartbreaks. Tonight, I wish
only to capture what little things went past me before
the sun went down this fine day, lest they fade.

Gabrielle set down her fountain pen. She sat at her desk in underwear. In a moment, she rose and moved to the edge of a large wooden chest elevated sufficiently for the top to be more than waist high to her, even tall as she was. Draped over the chest, an exquisite nightgown, cotton for the most part, but sewn with silk in the bodice, and completed by a short peignoir over-jacket of satin one shade darker than the ivory gown over which it was to be worn. Extensive delicate embroidery embellished the jacket. The skirt flowed generously over the side of the chest to the floor.

She appreciated the gown for minutes, touching it tenderly with long fingers, and then returned to her writing.

I saw four finches in one tree early in the morning.
There had never been finches there, I am sure. Two
pair live there now. I drew them with pastels, quickly,
regardless of all else destined for me this day. Their
music filled my heart. They flitted, though I sang softly
to them that all was well. It will be good luck if they
are still to be found tomorrow.

She replaced the pen in her hand with a hairbrush, meeting her eyes in the mirror occasionally while attending to her tresses. The cut she wore left long falls past her shoulders. These were already free, and she brushed them into order. Several braids of different length and girth descended along the left side of her face, some composed of the furthest forward tresses, two others spaced back near her ear. She approved of this effect and did not disturb it. Her hair gleamed golden, clean, and light as a mythical angel's basking in the young sun.

> I received a beautiful card today. It was from a young man who pursued me four years ago. His poem today was perfect, neither possessive nor bitter. For this I honor him, though I may not write back. His name was Stephan, with black hair I remember as dangerously captivating.

She stood in the middle of the small room and removed her undergarments. She shifted a chair aside so it would not obstruct her view in the mirror and adjusted the lighting. Spinning, she considered all views. Her skin glowed, smooth and fine. Her stance revealed the posture of French aristocracy, a delightful hand-me-down from ancestors. The wide, sensual mouth, from whom did that come?

And a gently curving torso? Gabrielle had always felt her breasts suitable, even with the happy chiding of a friend possessing abundance, who once admitted envy, with also perhaps an appetite.

She believed her hips to be glorious, having been told. What does a man see there? She laughed, thinking of more than one blubbering answer attempting to discover this riddle's key, since she also saw the gentle oval-like curve, perhaps sensed the the tug men felt, and in the end knew no more than that.

> The taste of a black raspberry. Today I popped one in my mouth for the first time. It was in the kitchen and Marie was helping me discover the difference between blackberries and black raspberries. I was easily persuaded to continue eating them until the lesson was gained. But what is the taste of the new fruit? I wish I could draw how it tasted. The last color I would use would be black.

With gentleness, she dressed herself in the immaculate gown. It fell into place like a dream. She made her hair fall just as she imagined it would, pouring over her shoulders. There was a satin ribbon at the waist, the only way to gather the gown. She observed closely in the mirror the two effects, tied and revealing her hip, or loose, hanging down tantalizingly, suggesting freedom underneath. This last effect was heightened by the easy ability for light to pass through the fine fabric and do its own defining. She decided to pull the ribbon and make a bow at her side.

> So many things I would have drawn today. Flowers, certainly. But to draw their fragrance? So too the laughter of children. This I heard many times. And in the eyes of those very close, those friends who would sing me happiness? This perhaps I will capture someday. And when I am old? My art would be complete if I could show with it the piercing joy I felt when he took my hand, never to let it go again.

Gabrielle slipped the soft satin jacket over her shoulders. She appraised herself in the mirror for the final time, turning this way and that, her bare feet arching with the hem of the gown spilling past. Finally, she walked close to the mirror to look straight into her shining eyes, and offered a prayer ...

"Ma chère grand-maman, je t'envoie une chanson au fond d'un cœur débordant. A ce moment-là, je porte ta robe, la même que tu a porté ta première fois il y a soixante-treize ans. Ah, que je sois courageuse dans l'amour comme tu étais! Aide-moi, grand-maman, de lui honorer toujours comme il faut. Mais surtout permet-moi de prendre ce lit comme le mien aussi, comme tu m'as instruit. Je t'embrasse. Je t'aime. Je prie à toi, où que tu sois au ciel."

"Oh, my dearest Grandmama, I send you a song from my happy young heart. I am wearing your gown now, the gown of your first night seventy-three years ago. Make me fierce in love as you were. Help me never honor him less than a man deserves. But let me take this bed for mine, as well, as you taught me. I love you and pray to you in heaven."

A look of serenity settled over Gabrielle's fine visage, with a glimmer in her eyes, nonetheless. With certainty, she reached her hand for the door of the dressing room and walked into her new life.

Video of Gabrielle's Prayer:
https://johncaeden.com/prayer.html

emperors of separate domains

On a terrace eighteen stories above the streets of Denver, he considered his world: no financial trouble on the horizon – happily and gainfully employed – an outstanding automobile parked below – extended family intact and lively – no physical worries per recent checkup – friends thinking him funny and fine. These satisfying things he savored in the pleasure of a cold sunny morning breaking over the city, with breezes carrying the scents of autumn.

And in the apartment behind him, in his bedroom, in his bed? A woman.

The right woman.

Six months they had danced the dance, sure of attraction, wary of the plunge. Their carefulness was not timidity – it was respect for the all-in stakes mating deserved, the conviction of which both considered themselves permanently afflicted.

Last night, however, when he dropped her at her car after their first serious date in two weeks, she trailed him home, knocked on the door seconds behind his arrival, swept into the living room, clasped his hand, and without a word led him into the bedroom.

He hoped he would forgive himself for not making the move. If not, living with the shame would be shamefully easy, his insides said.

He slipped in from the terrace and took a position in a chair near the bed. His lover lay sleeping halfway under the blue sheets on her belly, arms thrown out to either side. This woman – so strong in the night. He evoked the power in her kissing, her assertive touches, her physicality in lovemaking. The thrill in knowing she would bring fire to bed was so rich, it made him queasy. Measured breathing only partly succeeded in keeping sumptuousness under control.

"Oh, man," he heard her moan. "Man, wow."

"Yeah, that's right," he said.

She sat up, bringing bare legs over the edge of the bed, neatly wrapping the sheet around her torso. Her short hair looked wonderful with its smart city cut, even if rumpled. There was sleep in her face, but in her eyes the sun had already risen. She smiled.

"Hello."

"Hello."

"I've really done it now, haven't I?" she said.

"Yes."

"You didn't put up a fight, and now we've ruined our friendship with sex."

"Yes. Get your things and leave."

"I don't have any things here," she said quickly.

"Get your clothes and leave and we'll pretend this never happened."

"But if we sex-break-up, can we still be

friends?"

"No."

"Then guess what? You are stuck with me."

He didn't throw a comeback – it felt too good to let that last line hang in the air.

She tossed her head. "Ay-yi-yi-yi-yi, how many damn times did we say, 'I love you' last night, for crying out loud?"

"In so many words?" he asked.

She nodded.

"That can't be taken back?"

She nodded again, squinting in mock pain.

"We pushed out into the open ocean and sailed past the point of no return."

"Damn!" Moaning, she buried her face in her hands. He could see the glint in her eyes anyway, through slim fingers.

"So embarrassing."

"Completely."

They stood. Warm and fine in first embrace. A kiss. Hungry in it, searching and knowing, arousing and con

tent. New lovers have no reason to stop any kiss. This makes them often do so. They are infinite anyway.

The flow ran fast and far all morning. The shower they shared was full of intimacies of touch, first time here, first time like that, first time when I am yours and yours is mine. This ended on the bed where the taking went beyond that of the night, possessive taking, even as each found the other free. Free and taken, how could both be true for both? In lovemaking was the place to ask.

Then food, with laughing and teasing and bright eyes shining over apricot jam and some tea that tasted smoky.

"This is the best damn toast in the world," she said.

"Not as good as this yogurt."

"This meal has electrified our taste buds. This tea. What the hell kind of tea is this, anyway?"

"Lapsang Souchong."

"Lapsang Souchong," she sing-songed nicely.

"This must be our song!"

"Lapsang Souchong. Lapsang Souchong."

"Let's go to China and get some."

They quieted then, sipping the tea, eating slices of ripe pear, reveling in the peace and portent of each second. Then, he could not hold back.

"This is really happening."

Her smile came out, small, quiet, and tender. "I'm lost, like a fool," she whispered.

They sat in a chair and kissed. An hour went by without a spoken word. There was nothing their mouths did not know after that, possibly the closest intimacy of all since the sun went down the night before. Sometimes they kissed with eyes open. She was the leader in this practice. She could afford to let him see all the way in, apparently.

"Should we go back to just friends?" she asked, sardonically.

"No."

"Could we try sex only, no emotions?"

"No."

"Damn."

And tears. They began during slow coupling. He remained inside her body when she cried. He held her close until she passed to the end of it.

"I've given myself so completely to you," she whispered, looking in his eyes.

"Yes."

"I didn't know it would be this much."

"I'm going to ask for more."

Later they dressed, warm trousers and clean shirts, walking shoes. Jackets were required – autumn was asserting itself. She fitted a soft black hat on her head, one with shape and style, and they jumped out into the cold Colorado afternoon. The air stung going in their lungs, 'like the first breath of life,' they agreed, walking through fallen rusty leaves in Washington Park, with little fogs of mist on each breath.

At the far end of the park, he guided her to the section where the best trees stood, gigantic oaks, Methuselahs, placed far enough apart to seem like emperors of separate domains. He stopped her there.

"This is a honeymoon."

"Yes." She nodded, mouth set in certainty.

"I'm happy about it," he said.

"Yes."

"Married people have the assurance of marriage, though," he added.

"Oh."

"Do you want me to slow down?"

"No," she said. "Say it."

"A honeymoon will end. They have their life plans. Hopefully another honeymoon comes along."

"They'd better damn come along damn often," she said, making a perturbed smirk of her mouth around her favorite word.

"We should make every weekend a honeymoon," he said.

"Don't ever forget you said that."

He let a moment pass. He felt immensely buoyed by her character, her behavior. There was no panic, no grasping either way. Clearly, she sensed he was not done, and waited calmly for him to finish. Extraordinary. He was right about one thing – she had courage.

"Do you think we started a marriage last night?" he asked. "Not just a huge love affair, but a marriage?"

"Yes."

"We've only known each other six months," he said. "Maybe it's love and sex but not marriage."

"Too late. It's already all three. And more than," she said with discovered happiness.

Then she turned serious.

"Or nothing."

He held his breath. He could not even blink with the peril. She looked deep in his eyes. "I'm already past lovers and married and honeymoon. I want more. We can't be just sleeping together or in a marriage. Not if I'm going to give myself like that. I can't let you in my body like that and reaching down inside my emotions like that and still hold anything back. So, you have to give me everything, too. That's my word. I have to go all the way. One heart and one flesh. You have to tell me right now if you'll go all the way."

Everything – or nothing. With an inside shock he knew they had blasted away all options to hedge. It focused his will.

Under the stupendous oaks he loved, in the cold clear afternoon, with the beauty and strength to risk in a woman standing in front of him, all came to an end. Lesser things faded and fell.

"All the way and never come back?"

"Yes."

"Then yes. Yes."

fall out to the last strand

ImAngie103: Hello? Maddie? I'm here now
ImAngie103: Hello?
ImAngie103: **buzz**
MadNotSad: There you are. Where have you been?
ImAngie103: Couldn't help it. The mom kept me afk with stupid chores. is ne1 there yet?
MadNotSad: I've been IMing you for almost hour. nope, nobody yet
ImAngie103: She made me do part of the lndry room project for painting
MadNotSad: no answer if you call your house ya know. and ur cell straight to VM
ImAngie103: I had to use this scrape thing and now its all in my hair. Yeah, she puts my cell to only VM so we don't even hear the calls   ::::screaming::::
MadNotSad: gross
ImAngie103: SHE STILL HAS MY CELL damn. I still have this laptop, mother, so ha ha ha
MadNotSad: Type Fast. :) But you're still coming right?????
ImAngie103: Made sure. TheMom will let me stay til 11 Leaving in 15 min
MadNotSad: Better than nothing
ImAngie103: I am screaming n ready to dance
MadNotSad: Does your mom torture you like that every fri?
ImAngie103: I swear she just doesn't like me to have fun
MadNotSad: maybe shes not having fun
ImAngie103: i lv her n all b this is freakin fri nite

fergdsake

ImAngie103: they both might not be having fun

MadNotSad: my prnts don't.

ImAngie103: i swear she is worse than the dad with the chores.

MadNotSad: lighten up why dont they

ImAngie103: they had fun on that raft trip

MadNotSad: oh yeah, last summer

ImAngie103: yup. i guess it was a good time, even my stupid brother liked it. hes at his friends house until tomorrow nite or else id be babysiting

MadNotSad: talk about bad hair tho

ImAngie103: OH YECH. no showers and wet all the time for a week. no thank you next year. but now that school started they are mean

MadNotSad: do you think they have sex?

ImAngie103: MAD YOU BAD BAD GIRL

MadNotSad: really, do they?

ImAngie103: o gross just to think about it, shut up

MadNotSad: what if theres no sex for parents

ImAngie103: i cant believe this conversation

MadNotSad: like after you and your brother fall asleep, down in the family room

ImAngie103: o no wash my ears that is sso disgusting

MadNotSad: i don't think mine do

ImAngie103: that's right. maybe once by accident, now don't ever bring this up again whats the matter with you girl

MadNotSad: uh oh, something just happened. angie, guess what

ImAngie103: You just got your grades by email and you got an A in french?

MadNotSad: O hilarius. Wanna wait now, smartass?

ImAngie103: he he he he! You got an F in french?

MadNotSad: LOL x 2. then no news about this boy who just drove up. Im watching him out window oh shit so cute

ImAngie103: Jason Wentworth?

MadNotSad: no
ImAngie103: Steve, that guy from the catholic school?
MadNotSad: no
ImAngie103: Madeline Barry you spill it right now
MadNotSad: Allen T. I swear and no lie
ImAngie103: OHMIGOD! Mad no lie do not lie I will kill you
MadNotSad: Allen Trasczinski
ImAngie103: OHMIGOD! OMG! over and out you keep hands off and don't tell him im coming. my hair
MadNotSad: better hurry up, he brought a girl with him. this partys started.
MadNotSad: angie?
MadNotSad: angie?
*** chat terminated ***

He watched the familiar form of his fourteen-year-old daughter as she dashed down the street, having been called to the window by the crash of the kitchen screen door. She was practically running and visibly irritated.

"You're making her walk?" he asked.

"It's only half a mile," his wife said. "I made her set up a ride home from Madeline's parents by eleven."

"Let me guess. She pitched you hard for a later curfew, and wanted you to drive her, but drop her a hundred yards away from the party?"

His wife nodded, showing her best wise smile to him. He laughed.

"By the power of parties with boys, thereby shall time for the old ones alone be duly and surely granted. May they make the most of it."

She seemed to think that perfectly droll, judging by her bright eyes. "Oh, we are old, aren't we," she intoned while coming close and slowly unbuttoning her sweater.

"Ancient."

She reached the bottom button but left the garment in place. Her hand bent gracefully up behind her neck and undid her hair with a small tug on a ribbon. Its deep black thickness spilled about her shoulders. She shook to make it fall out to the last strand. In the hush of their bedroom, this act made a sound, the softest whisper imaginable, like the sifting and settling of dust shaken from the moon when hearts pull on it from earth.

all the way to dessert

"What's a 'sweater girl'?"

Sam looked over at his great-grandson. "Where'd you hear that?"

"Well, someone said 'I'm no sweater girl.' What does that mean?"

He had little hope the boy would be generous with circumstantial details. Answer anyway.

"It's a term from the olden days, you know, the fifties."

"Sheesh. The nineteen fifties?"

"Yup, way back there." He was always amused how far removed his salad days seemed to this teenager, when to him it was immediate as yesterday. *These kids probably don't grow out of their salad days anymore – green is probably green, all the way to dessert.*

"Okay, what's it mean?"

"A sweater girl is a young lady who looks really good in a sweater, really good, because she's built on top and has a narrow waist."

"Oh."

"The sweaters we're talking about are pullovers with no buttons or anything, or they button in back. The way polite girls used to say it back then was 'shows off your figure.' Basically, you have to have big breasts, special bras, and not be shy to pull it off. It was the big famous way for girls to look back in the fifties."

"Okay."

That was it. His great-grandson was not going to say anything else, he was sure. He tried to work up some gratitude for the miracle of being asked in the first place.

They were arguing over who gets what.

"Listen, you're giving me a hard time, kid. The blonde's for me. Man, is she stacked."

"What if I want her?" Sam asked.

"Not for sale, now lay off," the other said, too rudely.

The two girls were talking in low voices thirty feet away. They glanced over. He locked eyes for a second with the slight one with wavy brown hair.

"I'm giving in this time."

His buddy stood up straight with a wise-guy smile. They sauntered over to the pair, offered their arms and went into the dance.

"You're Sam, right?" the brown-haired one said right away.

"Yes."

"I'm Margie. Margaret, but everyone calls me Margie."

"Is that what you like?"

"Yes."

"Okay, Margie it is."

"She's a big brain, ya know," the blonde girl

said as they took seats at their table. "Smarter than them college professsors."

Sam looked at his date. She was smiling slightly but shaking her head. "Yes, but can she do the Cha Cha Cha?"

"I'll try it if you do," said Sam.

"Okay." They smiled together. He was greatly relieved. The hard part was over, the ice was broken, she was not a disaster. He found himself on high ground. He was going to have a simple good time tonight, no expectations.

And so went his first evening at the side of the girl with the wavy brown hair. They talked much about simple things, but never in an ignorant way. He bought her two rum and Cokes, which lasted a considerable time, and she proved herself on the floor, doing a medium-cool jitterbug as well as the Cha-Cha. They whispered about their two companions, who seemed glued together on the floor and off, Margie holding the opinion that her friend 'was being too willing.' Sam did not say a word about that aspect, not inclined to follow that line of inquiry. He was conscious of Margie's diminutive body, its allure keeping up a drumbeat in his senses when holding her close, hand in hand, touching gently in front, during ballads.

That policy stuck while they walked to her house: her education, her professors, her dad, yes – anything more private, better left alone. They sat on a bench in one corner of her front porch finishing a point of conversation, comfortable in the clear evening air. A fine ache throbbed in his chest, the kind that seems to lift you off the ground.

"Margie, you're a swell dancer," he said. "I guess you can do the Cha Cha Cha."

She glanced away, then back over at him, the toss of her head jostling the wavy tresses. "I like the way you danced when the slow ones came on. Like that Patti Page song."

A shot of excitement ran up his back.

"Oh, I liked that too," he said. "I'll be asking you to dance the 'Tennessee Waltz' with me some time soon."

"That's a very sad and very beautiful song ..." She stopped short, looked down at her hands in her lap. "I'm not like my friend, you know."

"You don't have to say anything," he shot out immediately. "Don't say anything."

She looked up. "I don't have her blonde hair, and look how tall she is."

"She's a real bad dancer."

They both laughed. "How could you tell, Sam? She was draped all over your friend like an overcoat all night. You know, she's really a good kid, just sometimes she can't help herself." Then her voice and intonation slowed. "She'd never have to go one night a week without a date, if you know what I mean."

He nodded. "He's not actually my friend, Margie. He just gave me a ride to the dance."

She quieted. He waited. She looked right in his eyes.

"I don't have her figure."

She said it simply, her gaze steady and meaningful. It was only a second before he spoke, but it seemed an eternity.

"No, you have yours."

She stood up and offered her hand back to him. He came to her side, and they walked across the porch. He would have taken a small kiss. He would have taken no kiss. Instead, just before she opened the door and ended their first night together, she offered to him in her glowing eyes a look that took his breath away. It was that of a woman revealed, a woman capable of a gigantic love.

"Good night, Sam," she whispered.

"Good night, Margaret."

her mind had made

Half a mile inland from the northeast corner of Lake Erie, where it formed up into the Niagara River, light spilled out onto an alleyway from an aged building in an industrial pocket of Buffalo that happened to otherwise contain no all-night operations. Quiet prevailed, just before dawn.

In the deep night, a jet-heater, an air compressor, and occasionally the motorized traverse of an I-beam-tracked block and tackle had contributed to affairs inside the high-ceiling, one-story brick building, once an auto machine shop, now the site of a much riskier undertaking.

In corners of the thirty-by-thirty-foot space stood assemblages of glass panes, small panels of window-like units, unframed sheets of plate, lengths of stainless steel tubing, and other welded and fastened metal shapes. Along the walls and on workbenches it was clear by lack of clutter that every extraneous item remained out of the way – everything extraneous to the construction of that which dominated the space.

In the center, on a twelve-foot square foundation designed to be moved by forklift or electric tug, a structure rose dramatically. Straight rigid members of metal angled from myriad anchor points in the base to reach upwards. Some connected to others where they happened to meet. Others tapered and terminated fourteen feet above the floor, seeming to shoot the sky. The geometry involved in the canting of these struts exemplified complex logarithmic order – it listened to a pulse and flow far deep in undercurrents.

Filling the metal forms of this three-dimensional skeleton: glass, clear, clean glass. There were great sheets of it, cut to be triangular, rhomboidal, some nearly eighty square feet. There were small inset panes, repeating, offset from one another by mere millimeters, set as overtones determined by an infinite harmonic series. There were narrow fillers between two not quite parallel struts. In many places, flat glass panes were set in arrays of variegated angles such that the eye suspended disbelief and saw arched lines, when not one curved edge obtained in this crystalline mammoth sculpture.

It was a piece to be walked around. A woman had been doing so for an hour. Her overalls were stained. They were torn, also, where the excess of one cuffed pant leg hung over steel-toed work boots. Curly hair, once held in place by a ponytail, now rebelled against constraint, frizzing and flying loose. Occasionally she attempted to push it in place with a hand rough from working in the cold, bruised from the physicality of her art, cut in more than one place.

She stopped at one corner of the sculpture,

considering it long, with no movement except the flickering of intense black eyes, searching. Then her gaze lowered, abandoning focus on the level of the physical. The eyes lost their outward fire, their searching stopped for a long slow time in silence. She was as still as the sculpture, rapt by its music in her mind's eye. Then, as in a dream, one hand moved from her side and rose, evocatively curved and supple, making expressive circular movements off to her side, connecting.

She straightened. The immense power of her concentration returned to the sculpture itself, the fact of it here on earth, on this factory floor, for the first time. The dark eyes grew fierce.

Quickly, purposefully, she turned off every light in the studio and shuttered the windows. The sculpture disappeared. She took up a position she knew would be of advantage shortly. All became still. In silence, fifteen minutes passed.

Then, she reached for a switch box nearby and activated its control. A sizable skylight revealed itself. The first rays of morning light entered the studio and glinted off the highest tip of the sculpture.

She stood in place for an hour while the earth rotated under the sun, watching its power captured in that which her mind had made.

It was a full-blown January thaw.

The sun asserted its dominance. The south-tending pressure on the arctic jet stream relinquished its hold, causing cold air to retreat north. Everything melted. The streets of Buffalo ran with rills, rivers, of melt-off. By tomorrow it would be down to the hibernating grass. Now liberated by the dazzling sun, water dripped and gurgled from rooftops, under snow drifts, beneath buried abandoned cars, in swollen streams whose voices had come alive.

Mila sloshed home through it.

In her happiness, she considered the grand meltdown a tribute in her honor. She gloried in it, sporting a wan smile as befits facing the sun in a high sky after an all night battle with fear, one that called on all her strength, departing the battlefield victorious, her adversary impotent, diminished, whimpering in the dingy alley outside her studio that guarded its exultant contents with pride.

Snow still lingered in the front yard of her house. She noted how dirty and granular it had become, crusty. She ascended the front steps, squashing some of it into puddles. A wave of fatigue hit inside the door. Within three minutes she had slipped under the corner of fresh sheets on her bed, within five had fallen asleep.

"What the hell is that great smell?"

The cook spun around. "Bacon!"

"I'm starving," she told him.

"Breakfast or lunch?"

"You'll make either?"

"Absolutely. I hope you slept well. I thought about calling home to check, but I didn't want to wake you, either."

"Oh Karl, I'm sorry, I should have called you at

school this morning. At least left a message."

"It's okay."

She padded across the kitchen. "Sorry," she said again as they embraced. She was sleepy and jumbled emotionally, but kissed him with confidence.

"It's so amazing outside," she said, moving out of his arms, peeking through one of the curtained windows. The sun was fully in charge out there. Everything was soaked and melting and sparkling.

"It took fifteen minutes extra to get home. Some intersections are really flooded."

"You know we'll see it on the news, at least one idiot in a pickup who thinks he can make it, and gets stuck," she said.

"I saw a few like that. Not even trucks, Volkswagens. You know those trestles on the West Side? Flooded."

He extracted from her the choice of breakfast, early afternoon though it was. Eggs and toast, then, plus coffee.

She grew silent, standing by the window. He was occupied. Eventually, all cooking noises ceased, and an appetizing plate landed at her spot at the table. She realized that with her wild curly hair, gigantic blue sweatshirt, bare legs with feet in purple socks planted on the hardwood floor, she must be a sight. She sensed him looking, amused with her insuppressible smile. The smile expanded.

"It's done," she said.

"Really?"

She nodded and moved slowly over to the table

like one in a dream. The smile kept growing. She sat across from him.

"Done."

"It's spectacular?"

"Yes."

"It's the greatest thing you've ever done?"

"Yes."

"And it's done?"

"Yes."

"Did you end up with the second design?"

"Oh, you don't even know. That second conceptualization died around midnight, about an hour after I called you. Karl, there's so much more."

"I see."

"I can't explain it. Everything happened in process. It went beyond." She loved him substantially – which was the only reason she verbalized even this much. The events of the deep night had grown new parts of her, raw organs and muscle that had just filled out. This hurt. It thrilled.

"Do you have to go back?" she asked.

"No. No class this afternoon. Cancelled. I sent my class an assignment by email. The university is closing down. I'm telling you, this is no joke. The river and lake are still frozen, so the storm drains are backing up."

"Come with me."

"Mila, you're going back there?"

"I have to. It's not a choice. Even if I have to swim, I'll be gone in thirty minutes."

"Guess I'd better go. Save you from

drowning."

She smiled gently at his sardonic joke, but in a moment the smile blossomed wide, took on a life of its own. Her eyes welled over and her face filled with a piercing, ingenuous joy. She cared not that her lover saw. She was safe here, in her home, in the presence of he who she believed would not chide, not gainsay her emotion. She let many things come true in her face, then. Her tears flowed not from the failing of her soul, but only from the opposite of pain – from naked radiance.

"I've never seen anything so beautiful in my life," he whispered.

More of Mila may be discovered by reading *The White Sky.*
thewhitesky.com

since day one

W hatever you do, don't ask him."

"Why not?" asked Simone.

"You give your power away," said her friend. "He has to ask you."

"Wait. We girls have the power because we don't ask for what we want?"

"Yes."

"That's twisted."

"Don't ask him."

They exited the girl's bathroom and merged into the throng. The door to last period, AP English Lit, arrived immediately. She turned in, her girlfriend speeding down the hall on a different adventure. The class began to settle, with Mr. Andrewjeski writing something on the black board.

She took her seat right behind the boy. They missed glances as she passed by. That was accidental, though, and did not hinder the go-impulse for her plan.

Then, Shakespeare erupted.

He caught up to her outside school.

"Wait, Simone, you drop a sealed note with 'do

not open until you ask me if you can' on my desk and run away?"

"Yes," she said.

"What the hell?"

"I want to see if you're going to leave it sealed, and if you'll ask me."

"I don't get it."

That was disappointing.

"That's disappointing, Alex. Try something else."

He dangled the letter in his hand. It was sealed. "I'm not going to ask a girl permission."

"Strike one."

"I'm not throwing this thing back in your face, though, right, Simone?"

"That's better."

"Wait ... strike one ... you think I'm going for you?" he asked.

"Yes."

"No."

"Yes."

He stood up straight, took a glance down at the note, then stared her down. In one instant she saw his contrarian visage turn into ambition – with a faint surprised tint as if he stupidly realized it had been there all along and was now trying to hide it. It was so *boy*, so comical.

"So, I'm not on any base and I already have strike one?"

"Yes."

"But I can't rip this thing open unless I ask you to let me?"

"Correct," she said.

"I thought you had a boyfriend."

"Might."

"So, you're cheating."

"No. He and I are not serious. He's more of a friend."

"Uh-oh, you put boys in the friend zone?"

"He wandered in there."

She absorbed his gaze pressing forward and his body slipping a few inches closer. His scent came across.

"I have a girlfriend," he said.

"Really. A real girlfriend. A girl."

"Yes."

"And you *have* her?"

"Yes."

"Are you sure?"

"She's in another school. You don't know her. Luna."

"Is Luna as smart as us?"

"You think you're smart?" he asked.

"You know we both are. Smarter than any other kid in this school. Smart enough to figure out what the hell Hamlet is actually saying. If you'd raise your hand more, you could try proving you're as smart as I am."

"I know you're smart," he said. "You show off all the time."

"So, what about Luna?"

"She's ... smart."

"Really?"

"She's attractive."

"That's nearly strike two. Maybe a foul ball."

"She's taller than you, and she let me kiss her

for five minutes on our first date last week."

"Strike two. That sounds like casual sex, not even a date, let alone 'girlfriend.' Looks like we'll have to get tested before I kiss you."

"You can't catch anything by kissing."

"I'll have to at least make you obliterate Luna with mouthwash. At least."

"So, how long have you been sitting there behind me in English, putting your spells down the back of my shirt? I can feel them now, since you've stirred this up."

"Since day one. Just little ones at first."

"Well, it's November. So, for three months?"

"Yep," she said. "All this time you didn't feel them. You never looked at me that way. Not once. I don't think you thought of me at night even one time."

Things stood still a moment. Except in their eyes. Then he lifted the envelope.

"Can I open it?"

"No."

She turned and walked away.

He ignored her in class next day. She ignored back. They walked away in different directions outside the classroom. Her girlfriend came rushing up.

"Simone, what did you do?"

"Huh?"

"Here." She thrust an envelope forward. "Alex told me to give it to you, and if I opened it, he'd kill me. He was all worked up. What did you do to him?"

It had his scrawl on it, "do not open unless you ask my permission."

Alex showed up at her house, uninvited. He had to answer to her mother as Simone came to the door. The young adults walked out into the front yard, staying public. Each carried their letter.

"May I?" she asked.

"Yes. May I?"

"Yes."

They tore open the notes and read them one at a time out loud ...

One note said: *Yes.*

The other: *Will you go see The Twelfth Night with me, like a date?*

see the world in color

A month after Reina turned eleven, a near-miss predation incident frightened her parents to the root. Previous lesser occurrences had raised alarms, but this one exposed the fragility of their daughter's very existence. Her mother moved from high-warrior focus during the chaotic events, to exhaustive sobbing when it was over, and now to icy confrontation.

"This will continue," she said with steel in her eyes.

"We're not moving," Reina's father replied.

"We should move farther out."

"I won't take her school away," he insisted.

A fateful pause. He watched a look of ferocity take shape in the face of the woman he loved.

"If one of these animals kills her, she won't be attending school."

He was smart enough – and terrified enough – to not mitigate this truth. Within a week they had restructured their finances to precipitate a budget for a building adjacent the school in which to relocate their flower business, for consultation and ongoing services of the strongest personal security firm in Florida – and for a gun.

Over the next decade, the engine of this wrenching dilemma only accelerated. The eleven-year-old who was so beautiful the word "angel" sprang to the lips at every encounter, became a woman of lissome, sensitive movement with a visage of tender loveliness that stopped one's breath.

On her twenty-fourth birthday, having declined three serious contract offers for modeling and film, she graduated first in class with an advanced degree in structural engineering from Georgia Tech. One year later she completed her MBA.

Every time the floor became aware of a new-hire prospect's interview, the office ran a gamble. Some thought it made a difference, boy/girl. This was not born out statistically. The participants being naturally inclined toward visualization of math, the bets were influenced by a matrix grid, the x-axis standing for "degree of stunned at first sight of the boss" and the y-axis for "candidate's despair over criteria for hiring." Before betting, all were eager to consult this chart constructed by Sarah, who held down the front office. She asked the same question of every candidate emerging from the interview, "How did it go?" and pinned up the graph and her estimation of hire on the lunchroom wall.

Sarah held in one sense the highest position in the firm – she was the only one to claim a modicum of personal traction with her stoic brilliant employer. The front desk was her day job. She was an artist, a watercolorist, jocularly embedded in a sea of advanced left brains. Reina had arranged this on purpose.

"You don't mind if I don't know a thing about building a building?" Sarah had asked at her interview.

"In your dreams, do you see the world in color?" asked Reina.

Sarah nodded, arrested by the poetic question and the intense eyes holding hers.

"I'm betting you'll help an architect feel assured of our competence, feel less nervous about spending a million of his client's money with us for engineering design. What if that's your job?"

"That would be ... ideal, actually."

"Sometimes I don't put them at ease."

Sarah's eyebrows went up. 'Guess not,' they seemed to say.

"Find out why we are the best in the world," Reina continued. "Hold on to that all day long. Keep your painter life separate. Leave the job here when you go home. You are hired."

A year later, when the interview rating thing caught on, one of the engineers asked Sarah to post her own hire matrix. She drew two lines on a piece of paper and put a star in the uppermost left-hand corner; 100% stunned by her boss' appearance, 0% intimidated.

In the wake of an enormous project overseas, Reina carved out a week in Miami before dropping back in. Her mother welcomed her with comforts, affection, and favorite foods. As usual the elder only brought up small things at first. Likewise, on the other side of the table with her father. They knew enough to await unfolding. They listened to their daughter's account of Italy and Southern France, brought her to the beach for days of sun and open air, and caught her up to speed on their flower enterprise, now on the level of serious agriculture spread out on a complex of fields and greenhouses over one hundred acres. The retail outlet remained prosperous, still located adjacent the school in Miami.

On the fourth day, the two women spent an hour wrist-deep in the soil of the family's personal tulip beds. They had been quietly planting for an hour.

"How do I seem?" Reina unexpectedly asked.

The older woman planted two more bulbs and came to a stop, kneeling across from the other.

"I'm keeping my promise. I'll never say I'm waiting for your smile to come out."

Reina nodded once.

"You know I can see inside, though."

"Yes."

"You seem whole. But there are hurts."

"Yes."

"Recent ones."

"Yes."

The mother said nothing more. She just held the gaze of the exquisite female who had come from her, offering unconditional acceptance. They resumed planting.

During her years of nurturing, she had to pass through concern over the ferocity of the child's intellect, a relentless focus manifested with iron stoicism. She even had to fend off professionals signaling abnormality about it – they were alarmed by the unwavering eyes, the subtle and unsmiling expression, the equanimity of a wise and settled scholar in an eight-year-old. When one went too far, and the whole family knew it, she delivered a now famous line cherished by the three: "You're just wigged out because you can't make her laugh."

Then there were the boys. If ever heartbreak were self-inflicted, the Alvarez front porch was the scene of ruin a hundred times. That Reina never gave an ounce of encouragement or tease did not reduce the carnage.

Worried, the parents made sure to force a conversation between sexual ripening and the day she left for college. The clear green eyes held both of theirs and hid nothing. She accepted all expressions of concern. She waited until they finished, then told them, "You showed me what it is to love – I see it in you every day. My heart is not closed. It will never be. But one of them has to say the right thing for me to give it. And he has to not see me, but not not see me."

Stunned, the elders absorbed this uneasily. The conversation was over. The enormity of the burden on the soul of this extraordinary creature made them hold each other close that night and whisper strengths to keep fear at bay.

~~~~~

"Hello?"

"Miss Alvarez?"

"Yes."

"My name is Korda, Rhys Korda. I'm calling you about a project."

"Are you an architect?"

"No. I have not engaged an architect yet, but I hope to get a chance to explain why I'm establishing the structural engineering first. It's a good reason. Can I have ten minutes of your time?"

"Yes. Let me hear it and we can decide how to proceed. But how did you happen to call me? And how did you get past Sarah?"

Reina permitted Sarah to pass "interesting and odd" calls straight through, with no preliminary.

"I told her I was starting something great and I had a million dollars in my pocket for this call."

"That was enough?"

"No, not quite, although I made her laugh."

"Yes."

"I told her five people said you were the best, and staffed only the best in the world. One was Bertocchi."

"Arturo Piero Bertocchi."

"Yes. I dropped that name on Sarah on purpose. Bertocchi does not want to be the architect for this project, but I asked him who the engineer was on his Lake Orinda complex. He was a little mysterious with me about you. But he said,

'Don't call anyone else.' He said it three times."

"Well, you've got my attention."

"I'm calling you from a dusty place, Miss Alvarez. It's the middle of nowhere. I want to make it the middle of somewhere."

"The moon?" she offered, deadpan.

That got a chuckle. "No," he told her. "This little town in Australia. Northern Territory, Australia, a little inland from the ocean. There's nothing here but dust."

"You're calling me from there?"

"Yes. Do you want to build something that will make a river flow here, so they can build an entire civilization? It's a desalinization plant."

"When will you be in the States again?"

"That's just it. I have a situation. I cannot leave Australia for at least six weeks. The window to stage this project opened suddenly, sooner than I guessed. Now the early political permissions are on the front burner, and I am handling the resistance daily. I also have a build in progress here, another separate project. I have to stay hands-on with that. Normally I would come to your office and make a detailed presentation. However, I have to secure my team well ahead. Now, in fact. So, I am asking for a business appointment to put this picture in your head, but it has to be done remote. I'll send docs and then lay it out."

"I see."

"Will you take the meeting?"

"To make a river you must have a really big plant."

"Yes."

"How do you know this is feasible if you don't have the architect yet, and obviously no complete plans?"

"I've been studying this for seventeen years. Not a fantasy. I have the money."

"Yes, on the meeting, then. Your appointment can be immediately, right now if you are ready."

He laughed easily. "Can you tell who is wooing who in this conversation?"

"No, and I like it that way," she replied immediately, as calm as every moment of her entire life.

"We'll never tell the world who made the first move."

"Make me see the big picture," she said.

One by one, the engineers took notice of Reina on this call. They could see her through the glass wall of her office, the blinds of which were not closed. Standing and pacing – that was unusual enough. The phone call had already lasted twenty minutes – that was definitely note-worthy. Abruptly, she put the phone down and turned to look around. The engineers ducked. They were aware that Sarah and Sarah's assistant were being drawn in when the two went tearing across the floor.

After a while they saw the elegant form of their employer step around her desk, phone in hand. When she had been talking another astounding fifteen minutes, Sarah was seen spreading maps, papers and blueprints open on the desk and taking new instruction from Reina.

"Okay I see it," she spoke into the phone half an hour later, looking up from the papers on the table. "It's even bigger than I thought. But I'm distracted by the political pass. It's nagging me. Can't think straight. The Australians have killed these projects in the past a few times. Give me the reality."

"I have a beautiful circus getting ready to perform for the authorities in two days. There's only one more major hurdle in this first round, and it's provincial, not national. At the meeting will be my guys."

"Your guys?"

"I'll stay in the background. There will be five people in front of the commissioners, a farmer from the interior, an entrepreneur from this damned town, and three Aboriginals. They are all my friends. One is 80 years old, the major chief in North Australia, the second a twelve-year-old girl, the third one of the giants of the national legislature, a real genius for the nation. He's famous. One by one they are going to say, 'We want the water'."

"What's the girl's name?"

"Arnurna Bukurnidja."

Reina paused. She never paused. Then, "That started out to be a test, but then I cared."

"Always test me," he said.

She paused again.

Then, "Will it work?"

"Here's our tag line to the bureaucrats, are you ready?"

"Yes."

By this time, more than an hour into the call, two engineers and Sarah had stopped working altogether and were watching with fascination. Abruptly, Reina bent back and a brilliant smile lit her face. Through the glass they heard a shriek of laughter. She came upright, shook her head and body left and right, pulling loose her silken hair, and to their astonishment kicked off a shoe which went flying across the office to smack against an outside plate glass window. She was so beautiful in her abandon it hurt the heart.

Two engineers took a step back.

"Whoa," whispered one. "Should we be afraid?"

Before she spoke, they saw in Sarah's liquid eyes the answer ...

"No."

Reina kicked off the other shoe.

"Say it again."

"Make the ocean sweet and the land will bloom ..." and they shouted together "... or you are fucking idiots."

Out in the drafting room they heard it. They saw Reina doubled over with laughter again, in her two-thousand-dollar suit and stockinged feet. The entire firm went into collective happy shock and all work ground to a halt.

"You can't say 'fucking' to the regulators."

"We'll give them the cleaned-up version. We're printing banners. 'Make the Ocean Sweet and the Land Will Bloom.' When I get my guys outside, we'll start up the swearing version again while we have a beer."

"What about Arnurna's tender ears?"

"She's Indigenous, but she's Australian. I can honestly say it's too late, she thinks that word is hilarious."

"Well, Mr. Korda, we need the next meeting. Serious engineering meeting."

"Yes," he said.

"Is it preparatory for a request for quotation or a working meeting on contract?"

"Have you ever had a structural failure or disappointed client?" he asked.

"No."

"Can you rally resources in a window four months from now through a year from now?"

"Yes."

"Since I'm engaging you prior, will you help me choose the architect?"

"Yes, I know who I am going to name first."

"Then price no object on fair contract. I'm offering you this project."

"Okay," she said simply, back in her fully firm quietness.

"You have to personally lead your team, Miss Alvarez, that's a condition."

"Yes."

"All kidding aside, this preliminary permission to proceed is very easy, but the real green light will be contingent on assurances on the reactors. I will need you to make the safety case and help us make the environmental case."

"I've already been through that with Bertocchi."

"Yes, he told me. He said you made an

enormous impression in Italy."

"Yes," she said. With spin on it.

"How many times has a corner of your mind started to visualize a journey to Australia in the last hour for our foundational interaction?"

"Two or three times. If you were in the States, we would be meeting tomorrow."

"When can you be here?"

"Four days. I'll bring two people."

"That's an expense of the project and you will bill us. I am wiring a good-faith retainer for fifty thousand U.S. to you tomorrow."

"Even before your circus meeting in the province?"

"Yes."

"Okay."

"Tell your people they will be getting dusty," he warned.

"You mentioned beer, so you must have it there."

"Someday, we'll all swim in a huge freshwater lake right where I'm standing. It's all about concrete and osmosis systems and atomic reactors, but then those things fade into the background, and you are left with flowers and that young girl swimming."

"Do your visionary ways get you into trouble?"

"Visionary." He seemed taken aback by that word.

"Yes. Do you have trouble with people not taking you seriously?"

"Yes," he said. "You have trouble with that too."

"Yes. You can't let it stop you," she said with determination.

"Is your trouble that people dismiss you because you are a woman?"

"No."

"Can I ask you when we meet?"

"Yes. Actually, you'll see it the moment we meet. What brings me trouble."

"Miss Alvarez, there is something you need to know about me."

"What is it?"

"I am blind."

most ardent of all

The storm opened overhead. A slow mover, no wind, so the rain poured straight down, heavy and loud. Peering out the big bay window, he saw pools forming where low points in the grassy yard trapped the runoff. How must it sound pelting the roof of the greenhouse, and would she wait it out in there?

He wanted a fire. With kindling and dry oak laid up near the fireplace, he set a fine blaze going. With it came satisfaction, the appreciation of fire's heat countering cool misty air rolling across the floor from open windows – storm and shelter simultaneously.

Through the downpour, the sound of a door slamming and a high-pitched squeal drew his attention. He walked out onto the porch with towel in hand to watch her run across the yard, swearing and laughing. He met her down a few steps and threw the towel over her head. They hurried inside.

"Didn't you see it coming?" he asked.

"Guess so, but it was too fine in there this morning, absolutely perfect planting time, warm. The urge, had the damn urge to plant, you know?"

Having no such inclination, he denied knowing.

"Rite of spring," she said.

She pulled off her tee shirt, replacing it with a knit cotton sweater of abundant neck and sleeves, a little too big, powder blue. He dried her hair. They settled on the floor in front of the fire. She kept up a running story of seedlings and peat moss, and how rich the compost smelled, even extolling the aroma of decomposed horse manure. The greenhouse and its demands suited her – she radiated joy like a spring goddess with feet in mud.

She sat between his legs backed against his chest. They watched the fire while she talked about gardening triumphs and delights. They gauged the storm's intentions by the fierceness of the rain – it seemed to have nowhere to go, as neither did they.

Eventually, kisses. This pleasure merged them, two independent people, well situated each in the world and sure of themselves, physical affection dissolving anything extraneous to exposing the core of their bond, the courage to open the heart a reward for hard-won trust.

Sometimes they kissed with eyes open. Sometimes they would move back to say something hot or sweet or funny. One time she said, "My mouth is your mouth." He was known for letting go of her eyes to behold her lips for long seconds. If this went on for any time, she might let her tongue emerge to circle and make the lips wet, then tilt her head to offer her mouth like a delicious flower begging for the other to drink nectar.

And thus, the enjoyment of a splendid afternoon. They shifted positions occasionally. He threw more oak on the fire when needed. Sometimes they talked, sometimes only gazed at each other with honest eyes. Most ardent of all, though, the magnificent kisses.

There came a break in the downpour. She stood, gestured for him to follow, and led him out onto the porch of their house, an oasis of dry decking in a soaked world. The air seemed clean and new, smelled of woodland and earthy mystery, while the lowering sun glinted off everything wet. A breeze now – he saw it stir a lock of her hair, moving it across her shoulder against the pale blue sweater. Her face shone with simple determination and mounting joy. She looked young. It flashed across his mind that she had looked exactly so under a white veil when walking to him three years ago.

"The rite of spring," she said.

"What do you mean?"

"I was planting. I heard the storm coming. It was something else that made me stay out there."

"What was it?"

"I decided at dawn. I put my hands in the soil all morning to make sure I was right."

She looked in his eyes, very deep, all the way in.

"I'm ready to conceive our child now."

His mind opened like a white-hot nova. He looked silently into her soul for seconds and seconds more, her words becoming truer with each beat. No need to assent – he had been asking for over a year. Then she spoke.

"This weekend is the right time. I'm fertile right this minute."

Desire flooded his face and head, unlike any before. It flashed down his back into his pelvis. He became only her mate. His hand went to her wrist and took it firmly, leading her to the door of their house. At its threshold, he lifted her in his arms. He did not stop looking in her eyes while carrying her all the way to the back of the house where their bed waited, clean, dry, and beckoning.

wilder than the world

It began to get difficult to pick her way along the shore the closer she got to the headland. Rocky. Narrow. Crazy. Her fourteen-year-old determination escalated as with each step the music pouring from a house on the clifftop above grew louder, its crescendos gaining on the quiet lapping of the sea against the beach. The music was wilder than the world. It thundered and crashed and raced with purposeful frenzy up and down the keys of a piano that must have been terrified.

The girl slowed. Someone stood at the base of the cliff where the headland jutted out into the ocean – a woman, clad in a red evening gown that wrapped her erect body. An ethereal tangerine scarf twined about her neck and down, its endpoints flitting with the onshore breeze. The woman held two red shoes by the straps from her left hand.

The music escalated. The girl approached. The woman did not stir.

"What is that?" the girl asked.

"He is raging."

"What is it, though?"

"We don't know yet. It's not finished."

"We?"

"How old are you?"

"I'm fourteen. Are you writing the music?"

"No, he is. But it leads up to an aria for soprano. I must sing, then. Do you know what an aria is?"

The girl shook her head.

"A song. It's the moment in a drama when the heart breaks open and everything pours out. Everything stops while she sings her soul."

The girl showed a calm visage to the woman. If a fiction of a sea-cliff with someone fierce in a dress, bare feet in the sand, violent music pouring down on her shoulders, would be doubted in jaded cities – if encountered for real at the ocean's edge would frighten a girl less wild than the world.

They listened, still and silent. A calm interlude emerged from deep chords, pushing aside the torrent. In it, a tender melody blossomed, despite the threat of chaos and bitterness all around. Scintillating notes of the piano ascended, quieted, softened. The music paused, waiting.

"Right there?" asked the girl.

"Yes. There."

"What's in the aria?" the girl asked.

"My desire."

"You are asking to have him?"

"Yes. And to be taken."

"In real-life or song-life?" She rose taller, as deserving for challenges to a woman of power.

The woman let her face become fully naked.

The shoes clicked quietly at her side.
   "Both."
   "Will that happen?" the girl asked.
   "Yes. It will happen."
   "Why?"
   "He's almost in love with me."

john caedan

out into daylight

"Do you see them?"

"Wait a minute silly, you keep asking. Just wait."

"Maybe they won't come."

"Has Billy ever missed dinner in a long time?"

They giggled over that, bouncing around the room, twirling past each other, glancing out the second-floor front window impatiently, their bedroom window, that of eleven-year-old twin girls.

"Roller blade with his friends or dinner?" posed Kelly.

"Dinner."

"Basketball or dinner?"

"Dinner."

"Nintendo or dinner?"

"Dinner."

"But only just by a little, right?" Kelly added with more giggling and bouncing.

"What about homework and dinner?" Susan smirked sarcastically.

"Dinner," they screamed together.

"What about it's almost dinner and Jimmy comes over with tickets for Catlin McAndrew he got because his sister got grounded and they're trying to pretend they aren't going to a girl concert but they have to leave now because it'll take an hour to get there and let's go."

"And he'll miss dinner?"

"Can't wait for dinner."

"Catlin, but he'll eat hot dogs from 7-Eleven when they walk to the bus."

"I heard him playing that album three times last night."

"He loves her."

"Billy loves Catlin."

"I'm going to tell his girlfriend I'm going to tell his girlfriend."

Susan got up on the bed, like on stage, and belted it out.

"You're my sweetest star,
but I ain't gonna love you from afar.
If you want me to be ...
the one who sets you free ...
then boy look in my shining eyes, it's destiny."

Jumping down, Susan and Kelly sang the entire song through, loud, nearly on key. They acted out the dance moves of the video. Eventually this grew boring, and they returned to the window where they fell silent in renewed hope for action. It was growing dark.

Perfect timing. They saw Billy turn the corner a hundred yards away. He was walking with that same girl. Susan ran to turn out the light. They positioned themselves to see without being seen, the giggles nearly uncontrollable. They tried shushing each other into silence.

"She's got that hair band on again," said Susan. "I think he told her he likes it."

"Dubious," said Kelly. "I think she figured out he likes it on her own."

"Oh, all right."

"I wish I could hear what they're saying." Susan stamped with impatience over this flaw in the setup.

Billy and his friend stopped by the walkway to the house. They were still in conversation. Each carried several textbooks and notebooks in hand. The twins saw what they wholeheartedly expected, since it had occurred almost daily for the last week. The girl smiled gigantically, tossed her hair, laughed at something their brother said, did a cute goodbye flutter of her right hand, and resumed her way down the street. Billy came running up the walk.

The girls spun away from the window and scrambled across the bedroom. Just as they got to the hall, they heard the call from below for dinner, simultaneous with the slamming of the front door. They ran down, laughing and humming.

That evening it was Billy and his sisters and their grandparents. During the meal in the company of this unusual configuration of the family, the girls said not a word about their spying, lest teasing or probing make things change. They were hungry for information, nevertheless. Then, a miracle.

"William, I saw you with a young lady out front just now," said his grandfather.

Bill looked up from his potatoes and gravy.

"Yes?" was all he said, slowly.

"Well?"

"What do you mean, Granddad?"

"Perhaps you could start by telling me the young lady's name."

"She's just somebody from school."

"Well, fine. But tell me her name."

"Jane."

Reluctance shone in Billy's eyes, but also the resignation of one dragged out into daylight from failed secreting. The twins were sure – if it had been Mom or Dad, Billy would have put up more of a fight.

He took another shovel of potatoes.

"And is she in the same classes as you?"

"Not even one. She's a freshman and I'm a sophomore."

"Well, how do you know her?"

"From photography club. She's into digital images and video."

His grandmother looked over at him with a quizzical expression. The twins held their breath, wide-eyed and delighted by this windfall of information.

"She uses a camera with no film, Grandma. I like using black and white film and developing the prints myself."

"How can there be a camera with no film?" asked his mom's mom.

Billy launched into an explanation, dragging

the conversation significantly off point. He offered to show his grandmother all about it on the computer.

"Jane!" his grandfather interjected, leaning forward. "You know William, I'm surprised you didn't walk her to her house. It was getting dark."

"Granddad, I offered to do it a couple of days ago, she only lives two streets over, but she doesn't want me to."

"What about carrying her books?"

"Huh?"

"There's no such word as 'Huh'," shot out Kelly. "Mom said so."

"What about carrying her books?" Grandfather repeated.

William was speechless.

"Haven't your parents ever talked to you about courtesy toward girls?"

"Well, yeah, they have."

"What did they say?"

"Well, it's okay to do small things for a girl, if she says okay, it doesn't mean she can't do them herself, it's a way of making it special, being polite and all. And it doesn't mean I have to marry her." He got this information out, just barely, while clearly in shock. The girls giggled madly over the word 'marry.'

"My, my," said his grandmother. "That's better wisdom than I expected from my daughter, considering what I hear about things in this day and age. I guess she and your dad deserve their time away after all." She looked into her husband's eyes with a knowing smile.

"But Granddad," Billy erupted with a look of teen terror, "if I carry her books, everyone will think she's my girlfriend."

The entire table burst into laughter. The twins were beside themselves with eleven-year-old glee. After a long minute of embarrassment, Billy joined in, smiling self-consciously and kidding with Kelly and Susan about his relationship status.

"What if she won't let me?" he said with wide-eyed new alarm.

That just started the laughter and gentle kidding all over again. Young William had difficulty finishing his meal, but somehow, he managed.

Overlooking a narrow sand beach in the west of Jamaica, a lonely hotel cottage faced the sunset. Between afternoon rains, the calls of lovers had lifted over the sea through open windows, sometimes desperate or bellowing, sometimes keening as if cries of mating birds on the wing. There had been much laughter, as well.

The lovers lay in each other's arms now, inordinately awake, the press of satiated bodies not a soporific as might be expected after release – instead, a bloom of new arousal, their bower perfumed by sea breezes laden with hints of sweet florals burgeoning in warm wet soil.

The woman dared look deep in the eyes of the man. She saw his intent.

"Oh my God."

"Yes," he said.

"I don't even know where I am now," she cried in disbelief. "If I fly away again ..."

"Let me," he whispered, trailing a kiss across her shoulder.

"Oh my God."

"Let me."

She accepted his mouth on her body. Helplessly, she surrendered to a wonderful new ache blooming in her pelvis. What bonds remained of her attachment to the world seemed fragile as parting silk strands. There was one, though.

"The children ..." she whispered.

He did not flinch.

"They're in good hands," he said, and continued kissing her, melting her, loving her.

some odd explanation

So much for that bookcase.
He glanced from his piled-up crammed boxes to the nearly full shelves against the wall, back to the boxes. Too many books. He tossed three empties across the room while standing near the door. This is not even a matter of getting more shelves – no more room, period. Many could be replaced digitally, of course. Can you love them the same way?

Right behind, a quick triple knock startled him. He hardly had to move to open the door.

"Gina."

She glanced at him and strolled in without a word and no smile.

"Something's wrong," he said.

She shook her head.

"Seven-thirty tonight, right?" He could not have the time of their date screwed up, he was certain.

"Yes."

He walked close and looked in her eyes. Something made him not worry. In fact, he was fascinated with this femme even more than ever, welcomed some odd explanation.

"You look great," he said. She had pushed her hair to one side, the black lengths stayed by a blue clip. A touch of red tinged her lips. Jeans and a white crop top. *What more could a guy ask?*

She held his glance for a second, then seemed to pass a certain point. "Let's have a date now."

"Now?"

She moved close. Her person, her energy, her scent, came inside his space. He liked it. She poised her mouth inches from his.

"I'm starving for kisses."

She turned her head perfectly. Then – yes, yes, and yes.

No guy would ever say no to this. You do not. The slightly parted lips, limpid, yielding as he eased them open, then her seeking movements, the tip of her tongue alive and strong just there, begging to be matched with his. She did not attempt a full-blown sex kiss, but it hovered, ready if called.

They moved mouths apart.

"Wow, sexy girl."

"I feel sexy."

"Your mouth is amazing."

"Yours."

"You notice I'm not pulling you into the bedroom, though."

She nodded. He waited. She gathered herself. She took a few steps around his living room, then looked back at him.

"I thought we were pretty close the other

night," she said. "I want to go to bed with you. It's amazing we haven't yet, especially after Saturday, you had me wound up Saturday night. I mean, wound wound wound up. I thought you weren't supposed to go this far without having sex."

"Supposed?"

"Actually, I'm breaking all the girl rules by coming here unexpected and kissing you right off and talking this obvious. Chasing you."

"No girl rules, Gina. Only the truth."

She nodded again. "That's what's got me all bothered. You're not playing by the boy rules. For instance, any guy is supposed to take a kiss like that and get me naked as fast as possible."

"Gina."

"You don't seem worried someone might say you're not a real boy."

He laughed. He never felt more boy in his life. However, little did she know – he was already playing by the man rules.

"How much experience do you have in this, Gina?"

She blushed deeply. She took another nervous spin around his boxes and books on the floor.

"For someone heading toward twenty-five, hardly any with the real thing, the actual real thing," she said. "In fact, never. I don't know what I'm doing."

"You want to be my lover. For sex and more than sex."

"Yes."

"You can't be a lover if you're not in love. We

shouldn't have sex until we fall in love."

"No one thinks that."

He nodded. He walked over to the apartment door and opened it part way. He came back to the center of the room and faced her.

"I do," he said.

She looked at him silently.

"What time is our date?" he asked.

"Seven-thirty."

"Don't go out with me if you can't do it that way."

She nodded. He looked with longing at her mouth, delicious and provocative as ever, thinking there was a good chance he would never kiss it again. All the vivid memories of their fine date last Saturday came to a point, as did all the high qualities she possessed, but perhaps could not believe in.

He let her walk to the door without saying anything more. She looked back at him once and disappeared.

as by a waterfall

Ablessing that went with the job: bailiffs stay fit. So it proved for Sally, who held forth in Section Five of the Municipal Court in the City of Glendale, California. This court adjudicated offenses to the civil code, traffic infractions, landlord disputes, and the like. Sally was the enforcer inside and she ran a tight ship.

She once calculated that from end to end each day she averaged three miles of walking, not to mention standing, reaching, lifting, and the stairs. Add to this the physical requirement as an officer of the court to remain in great shape, plus twice-yearly mini trainings, very military-like, and it was no wonder she had no trouble staying toned. Her crisp uniform blouse never looked quite right – too much Sally where the designer had assumed slender arms should have been. She wore her long brown hair in a massive braid down her back and the belt of a sidearm high on her sturdy hip.

Sally's strength, and her reputation as a no-nonsense trooper, frequently came into play. Inevitably, there were hurts that could not be allayed by the judge's decisions, many made far worse, more piercing, and occasionally the odd defendant or plaintiff who would not take the court's decision as final. She was one to jump in early in response to recalcitrance. Her main technique was a firm verbal warning accompanied by swift escort through the swinging doors in the bar and halfway up the aisle. If the offender did not instantly comply, she postured a certain way to the judge, who warned loudly of a possible arrest for contempt, while she sustained the threat by fierce set of mouth. Even this was not the final modus of response – twice this year alone she had had to subdue men larger than her, forcing them to the floor, handcuffing them.

"Mom."
"Nope. It'll be dad."
"He was on yesterday."
"That's my bet and I'm stickin' to it."
"Okay ... whatever."
The two young adults made this wager every afternoon. Who would make dinner? The rhythm varied unpredictably. There was a ground rule of the bet, tough to honor, that neither would attempt to gather prior knowledge directly, although the gathering of collateral evidence was allowed.

"I want Mom, and those enchiladas with molé and sour cream," the male half said.

"Sorry, you lose," said the girl.

"There's sour cream in the fridge."

The other just shook her head and resumed the declining of French verbs. Her compatriot, a burly sophomore, reluctantly pulled another book from his little stack on the dining room table. During the next hour they only returned to the bet once and indulged in two distractions, a ten-minute music break and a quick snack of grapes, both permissible under the rules of the house. Their phones were on slumber, except for parental emergency texts, which woke both units. Otherwise, it was the inevitable uptake of yet another morsel of scholarly wisdom, the nutritious diet of early high school.

At four-oh-five, the front door flew open. The bet was settled.

In the house part way up the hills of Glendale, soft night settled in. Sally's final interplay with the teens went well. After solid closure with both, she walked upstairs with a degree of satisfaction in her countenance, the incremental reward for stewardship.

Her husband joined her in the bedroom. He had made dinner and been on duty with the young people all evening. There had been a minimal amount of contention, the occasional descent into callow self-centeredness, and bad, bad music endured for a while. But his offspring were happy young people when all was said, and he walked lightly as he closed down the house for the night.

"Everything okay?" he asked Sally.

"Daria wants to go to a play on Thursday night."

"I'm surprised she even asked."

"Well, she had her arguments ready," Sally explained. "It's a dress rehearsal for 'The Merchant of Venice,' it'll be over before 9:30, there's a boy she likes in it, and she'll get everything else done, etcetera."

They laughed over the ploy of their daughter's vectoring directly to Mom, preempting immediate rejection from Dad, who was on duty. The teens were under the illusion that Sally was a softie, a point of view that would have amused her employer.

They laughed over the irony of Sally listening to the assorted miscreants of Glendale making ludicrous excuses all day, only to face special pleading from a determined California girl at night.

They laughed over his attempt earlier to concoct her best recipe, the famous enchiladas. Her son had said, "An enchilada is an enchilada, bring 'em on," while Daria consented to partake strictly on a maintenance of life basis, which apparently necessitated but a few bites.

Sally had spent the evening in sweats and a white LAPD sweatshirt. Now, she kept moving around the bedroom as they spoke, a little restless. Gradually the news of the day was exhausted, and they grew quiet.

"Tonight's still my night," he said at last. Their agreement was to trade off, each signing on for two twenty-four-hour time slots each week, taking control of the house, the meals, the young adults, the details – the other could just coast. "How are you?" he asked.

She sat on the edge of the bed.

"Just wound up a little," she said, looking up at him.

"I suggest you allow me to untangle you." This was code between them. It referred to her hair.

"Well, you know, I was thinking the same thing."

He took her hand and eased her up to come into his arms for an embrace. They took their time about it, rocking, exploring with hands in small gestures, squeezing away the distancing a busy day out can impart.

"Something occurred to me when I got home at four o'clock today after grocery shopping," he said softly.

"What?"

He turned her around in his arms and hugged that way.

"There was an anxiety attack at work after lunch. It was over that rush job I told you about yesterday. The client started pushing. I could hear the meeting going on in the office next to me. There wasn't anything nasty or unfair, but something caused the job to get even more insane, moved the deadline up twenty-four hours."

"Can they do that?"

He unknotted the bottom section of Sally's braid and began separating the strands. Her hair was flexible and strong, with filaments of rust and gold twined among the rich brown.

"Well, they can't demand it, since that was not part of the original agreement, but they can ask in a very insistent way. Naturally, we bring up the various exigencies causing expedite charges, overtime coverage. Exigencies, that's the word Charlie likes to use."

"Oh, Charlie."

Her hair flowed in his fingers. He was carefully gentle when going after snarls here and there, in no hurry.

"Now, Sally, he's not a bad guy."

"He's got your job."

"That's just it, that's what I realized coming home today. And it's what you have to remember, sweet. He's got the job that I didn't take. When he came out of that meeting, Charlie was moving fast. It was three o'clock, and for all intents and purposes he was now booked for a double day, and it was only the middle of it. I saw Charlie and Jin making a list of action points and a list of people. They glanced at me."

"Uh-oh."

He was now moving through the tresses with his fingers like a comb. The full mane was spread across her shoulders, falling straight down from there, tapering at the small of her back. From being entwined all day it was kinky and wavy. This pleased his eye.

"I would have allowed them to ask, with no resentment. Months ago, I told Jin she could do that, as long as there wouldn't be repercussions if the answer were 'no.' But they didn't even come over to my desk."

"Really."

"I punched out at 3:30 on the dot. I was the only guy in the office who did. They may all still be there right now. I know Charlie is."

She spun around to face him. The hair went flying like the mane of a startled colt, making his breath catch in his throat. Sally's eyes were shiny. "And now here you are!"

"You got it!"

They were kissing, instantly. He moved his hands over her back, deluged as by a waterfall under the cascading hair, intoxicated by its sensuality across his fingers. After a delicious few minutes, Sally put her head on his shoulder.

"Did you feel guilty?"

"You mean 'guilty as charged'?"

She laughed at this courtroom reference.

"You know what I mean."

"I felt a pull. It pulled once or twice in the car. But they're not going to fire me, I produce as much in my thirty-five hours fixed as anyone else in fifty-five stretched and stressed. By four-thirty I was with the kids. No more pulls after that."

Sally moved away, her form backlit from a lamp on a night table. She arched her torso and tilted her head in a deliberate motion that caused her hair – with no help from her hands – to gather as one full mass, settling behind her shoulders, streaming down gloriously. She shook it.

"I don't want to wash it tonight, because I know you like it crinky and all."

He nodded, spellbound.

She turned half away. Putting her fingers at the hem of the sweatshirt she lifted it with crossing arms up and over her head, tugging it away and onto the floor. Some tresses spilled randomly across bare shoulders now. She stood still and held his eyes across the room.

He was only a step away from their closed bedroom door. Deliberately he moved back and locked it with a sharp flick of fingers. The room sizzled with electricity.

"It's still my night to be in charge," he said.

She nodded. The brown mane swayed. As he took his first step, she lifted her strong toned arms and invited him all the way in.

joy at sky's outpouring

After two hours of steady downfall, she slipped into satisfying acceptance – this was permanent snow. The skies showed no sign of losing their sullen gray density, even on the fringes of the dome. She required nothing but her nose for winter to predict more on the way.

It was impossible to miss the upset in the office, as with an hour to go in the day, traffic anxiety – always ready to jump the buzz anyway – now escalated close to hyperventilation. Some had already abandoned their stations. Her next-cubicle neighbor simply could not concentrate on anything else.

"This is getting really bad," he remarked peeking over the divider.

"This is Denver," she replied.

"It's wet snow. I'm out of here." His nose disappeared back over the wall and departure scurrying was plain to hear.

She picked up the phone. It took four calls before she achieved engagement on the other end – apparently weather flight had beset the entire metropolis.

Her contact turned out to hail from Cheektowaga, New York, a town in the path of the disgorging Lake Erie Effect, and the result was sardonic bonding repartee at the expense of the panicked.

Another result was the opportunity for serious presentation of value, display of character, and a sale of services. With one final joke about the driving wimps, she ended her workday with a congratulatory settling of the phone in its cradle, a few notes jotted on a pad, and quick data entry of a new subscriber into the system. When she did that, her commission running total updated in the corner of her monitor on a spreadsheet. That number looked good.

She stood up. There was not a sound in the place. Smiling and glancing out the window with a look of delighted anticipation, she sang out across the abandoned sales room.

"Let It Snow, Let It Snow, Let It Snow!"

You could not not make a snowball. She went easy on the pack and sent it hurling against the big front-facing window of their bedroom. She got the reaction hoped for.

"Hey!" she heard him yell.

Another one, a little harder.

"HEY!"

She had to laugh when he slid open the side panel and scowled out. His hair was still asleep, and her attack had put annoyance all over his groggy face.

"What the hell are you doing?" he cried, with a sweet edge to the anger. She laughed and aimed another white bomb at his head.

"I suppose you ordered this up special."

"The Weather Outside's Delightful," she replied.

"There was nothing on the ground when I went to sleep, what did you do?"

"I got bored. I called 9-1-1 and asked for the weather guy. He was bored. We whipped this up together."

She took a two-step stomp toward him to show off her foot gear. He gave out one of his short dubious laughs.

"Snowshoes?"

"There was no other way to get home. The river was frozen over with cars."

"Wait a minute, where's your car?"

"No car."

"You left your car at the office and walked two miles in this?"

"We don't call it walking," she corrected, stamping around the yard with practiced lift and stride. "Tramping."

Her face shone ruddy from having halted exertion, and the scarf thrown around hung down over the light ski jacket. She had shoved her ski cap into a pocket, and flakes were clinging to her thick dark hair. She looked as if thirty degrees more frost would be required even to make her notice.

"Come on out."

"No, you come in here."

"I cut across the golf course and the ducks are all stirred up. I'll race you to the fifth tee."

"I can't compete with this, especially that

gear."

"What, these simple pieces of deer leather?"

She stood on one leg and presented her giant footprint for inspection.

"Right, over an Aerospace-grade grid allowing for a super light Top-Trail frame and Flexi-Max toe crampon and costing seven hundred dollars."

"You've been reading catalogs again. Come on out. They only cost three hundred."

"I have to go to work in half an hour. I can't go dancin' with a snowshoe bunny."

"Call in with a weather delay. I need someone to have a snowball fight with."

"Oh cripe."

"We can march across to Bingley's. I'll have dinner and buy you breakfast."

"Cross country tramping to the bistro?"

"You need coffee, and don't you want a beautiful girl to talk to?"

"Well, I obviously can't get her into bed, damn it." He gave another quick scowl and slid the window closed.

She shuffled around to the south side of the house. How fortunate to be backed up against a school yard, its wide-open playfield ringed with cottonwoods, which now bravely held their arms aloft, though burdened. The fall increased. With no wind, it descended fast and thick. She let her breath quiet until the sound of flakes striking her jacket grew clearly audible, here in the lee of the house that buffered sounds from the street, the snow itself damping all noise, a blanket pulled around.

Stillness, with power surrounding. Innocent ethereal flakes, yes, but dramatically and relentlessly, tons of frozen water pouring from the sky. You can stand inside as if an engulfing waterfall, but let it strike your hair and upraised face.

Then, the onslaught renewed itself. It came so fast, so densely, she could soon see the trees only dimly, and the house not at all. The snow poured all around her body, burying the broad webbed shoes and the boots buckled into them. No wind, just a straight down storm. She laughed at the extremity of it, raising her arms in a gesture of surrender to the size of the world.

Eventually, someone came into view. He approached from the direction of the house, shuffling along with a gait like hers of this afternoon, if less skilled. This person was armored up, however, with wool and down and ski hats and big scarves and gloves. She kept laughing at the outrageous snow onslaught and the dubious arrival of someone less at home in winter, who nevertheless met her challenges.

"This is completely nuts!" He groaned with incredulous outrage, drawing near.

"I hope it gets worse."

"I know you think we're still going cross country in this."

"Your nose is already red."

"They'd find us in spring in a sand trap," he predicted dryly.

"And your car is grounded. Or should I say, buried."

She moved to him, raising her arms in joy at sky's outpouring. He pulled her close. In their private whiteout, they wrapped themselves around each other, laughing and tussling.

"I think I see an emergency shelter over there," he said. "They might have brandy. Or bourbon."

"Think we can make it?" she asked with brightness.

"Let's try before I have to make an igloo and save you."

"Right."

They made a trail toward the front porch of their house, while behind them the wet flakes filled their step marks.

One or two over-burdened limbs on the big cottonwoods slumped enough to spill the buildup. The sun's dim power failed the gray evening, but darkness did not stay the fall. The magnificent blizzard never stopped for seven more hours.

had touched his heart

Get in car, loosen tie.

This bang-bang ritual occurs every day, he realized, right here, right in the prime spot in the company parking lot, as if saying to the day, *you are dismissed.* All his employees' cars were gone, of course. The tie thing was the lock-down moment.

He did not turn on the sound. No ZZ Top, no Randy Newman, no Tom Petty. Blasting those boys was his fire-hose way of flushing the day – today he wanted the drain-away method. He cracked the window. Air flowed in, cool, yet with an aching thread of warmth woven through, the genuine article. It smelled fine. This is the payoff for enduring the interminable Denver winter – the astonishing relief of *Springtime in the Rockies.* Well, just downhill from them.

It passed through his mind that despite the loud pain of childbirth, a woman forgives it at first sight of her child. He was not quite so quick to quit. *If I must hate something that drags on for nine months, let it be winter.*

Another part of the closure ritual was the roll-in to the house's garage. Always check for her car

– parked there now as true most days this late. Before pressing the garage door closure button, he took a moment to view the final glint of the spring sun on the hill-rise just outside, and let the warm breeze falling down it touch his face.

Inside, warm but not bright. For some reason, he didn't call out, instead wound through to the living room to find her fixed in her favorite chair, legs pulled up.

"You okay?"

She nodded slowly, expressionless. He didn't exactly believe her, to say the least, and sat down a few feet away to wait it out.

"I can heat up some chili for you," she said. "Or that chicken stew my brother made."

He didn't respond.

"Is it cold out?" she asked.

"No, actually, it's warm," he said.

"I couldn't remember, when I got home."

"You were downtown today at that new school, right?"

"Yes, they called me on priority basis."

She was the mentor-at-large in the Metro area for various pre-school and toddler programs. It was not so much the children who needed her, but the adult staff. She could get a call to visit and observe, and zero in on anything missing in the environment. It was seldom a piece of equipment, rather a needed skill or gentle attitude adjustment imparted to young caretakers, helping them 'do their inside work.' She was the healing peace-bringer. The Queen of Calm, many secretly called her.

She had stopped talking, looking away into the middle distance. Just as he was about to say something, she turned the face he knew so well to him, the open, expressive, real-woman face, looking in his eyes, full of something big. This visage was beautiful on his soul.

She whispered.

"Something happened."

At 7:30, the children began arriving. At 7:50, James arrived. There was no other focus but James after that. He never stopped moving, from his intimidating bouncing-bouncing half-dance, to runs across the room, to shouts of nonsense. He bumped up into other children frequently and pushed a few times. It didn't take long for her to get it about James – she stopped looking at him and instead watched the two staff women reacting. They tried a few strategies, but James yanked away from them and took his chaos across the room. The boy was four years old.

After fifteen minutes, there was little abatement. She took the older staffer aside to ask about 'breakfast and sugar' and 'is this typical each day' and 'medication' and 'what else have you tried.' The upshot was, 'we don't know what to do.' She nodded and returned to the back of the room to watch a little longer.

James attempted a focus. There were long red rods and a wooden box involved. He kept failing the slow way, tried jamming, banging, and finally stomping. In the end, he ran over to the side of the room, grabbed a box of green and blue blocks, brought it back to his spot, and dumped it over the red-rod-box with a crash and scatter. Screaming with rage.

She had moved quietly near. She stood next to him when the blocks went flying, did not flinch, said nothing, touched nothing. James barely noticed her. He sat on the floor, rocking, calling out for juice. She sat down next to him just inside the edge of his space.

Gradually her presence began to irritate him. At first, he turned his back to her and started tossing the blocks. Several sailed into the space of other children, not accidentally. Then, James tried to provoke. He called her a name. He ran around her twice. He scooped up the double mess into the block box, jabbering loudly, pushing it against her knee.

She was unfazed but not unreachable – when he tried eye contact once or twice, there were her big brown ones, ready to hold his. James looked away, but fell to his knees next to her, jiggling, rocking, jerking, and calling out. Up to then, the boy had been bouncing off the wall, but the presence of so monolithic a soul, stoic in his storm, provoked his pain – now he was bouncing off the ceiling as well.

The vibrations in the young body accelerated. His eyes went wide, mouth open. It was not a scream, rather a growing wail. But no tears. He picked up another block with intention.

She sprang on him, took him by the arms, wrapped him up, pulled him to the ground, and surrounded him with firm strength. James squirmed and screamed and thrashed, pumping his small sneakered feet against her. He tried to break away. The clenching of muscles and hurting cries from his throat made the struggle sad. She just held her position over him and around him and let him flail.

Gradually, his struggle subsided. She did not change position, her envelopment complete and rock solid. James stopped crying out. Still, she did not move or release for the whole time of his long descent from fury.

Then, thankfully, a moment of surrender – the boy let go from inside out. He accepted her envelopment, her touch, her care. From the moment his breathing reached a peaceful rhythm, she sustained for a full half-minute more, cinching the certainty of it. When her intuition knew, she rose and released young James. He sat up and held her eyes. She could see the deeper guarding, the block at the closed center, but at least surrounding it now glowed a faint penumbra of warmth and life, a belt of emotion that would protect by serenity, not attack from raw rage.

During her telling, she had stood up to pace. He took a stance next to her, near the kitchen, near her plants, near happy things of their life.

"You didn't say a word?"

"No."

"What did he do?"

"James slowed way way down. He moved over to the side of the room and took out some paper. We thought he was going to draw or something.

But then, after about five minutes, he fell asleep. I moved him onto a rug and covered him."

"Wow."

"I held a confab with both women in that room. They had to ask, I knew they would, 'are we supposed to do that'?"

"Uh-oh. What did you say?"

"I just got on top of that question, said 'this was a big emergency'."

"I see."

"The younger one started to say something about 'no touching' so I ... well ... I had to give her a look."

"Oh no." He knew this look. It is correct, but it weighs four hundred pounds.

"It's okay. We have a moral obligation to protect the other children, and legal permission to restrain when needed. At the end of the day, we talked it out. We are all happy."

He hoped so.

"About an hour later, I was sitting near the front of the room having a few pieces of apple, watching the children, the children were so happy today, they could be happy, the difference in the room was huge, the others told me. James came walking through. He just came over near me to see what I was eating, he kind of brushed up against me, then he sat down, not too near, not too far. I cut him some apple and passed it over." Her face began to soften.

"I keep seeing his little feet with those great sneakers swaying back and forth beneath his chair, but gently, and he's nibbling away at the fruit."

He could see that too, in his mind's eye.

"He's a just a boy," she threw in, with a shrug and a gesture of the beautiful obvious.

She looked into his eyes. He saw tears coming. He made sure he was close to her – this was going to be a flood. Her head began to slowly move back and forth in disbelief.

"That's all they need. They just need to know we are there."

He took her in his arms for comfort and to let her release. She shuddered once, twice, then told him the thing that really loosed her feelings.

"I don't think any heart had touched his heart for a long long time."

Sometimes you arrive home to a glass of beer, sometimes a football game, sometimes a huge political discussion. A bowl of chili, for Pete's sake. This was his arms full of his powerful mate. This was the courageous core no one else saw, the love of his life, his *Real Emotional Girl*.

since girls will look

He dropped the cell phone on the kitchen tiles and kicked it across the room. If not already sitting on the floor, he would have collapsed down dramatically.

"I hope it's broken," he whispered bitterly, "so she can never call me again."

Alone in the stillness of the house as night came on, he sat in bitterness, back to a cabinet, slumped and dumped. From the slack mouth, irregular spasms of his torso, and bent head tracking back and forth in disbelief, there could be no doubt – sixteen-year-old cool stood no chance – this was a young man absorbing punishment.

After ten minutes more of poignant misery, a disturbance hinted he would be alone no longer – multiple young voices came floating up the driveway. They countered each other incessantly, and their owners must be walking fast, he could tell. There could be no mistake, there were many – and they were girls.

He glanced up once toward the hall exit from the kitchen to the stairs. No. No, for some perverse reason he must stay, delicious as it would be to slug up the stairway to continue indulging his aching heart in lonely silence. He struggled up, at least, staggered to the refrigerator, fetched out a quart of milk in a glass bottle, and struck a reasonable pose just as the front door flew open and five, actually five girls, all within two years of his age, burst with sheer zest into the house, breezed through the living room, and invaded the kitchen like ravenous killer honeybees swarming.

Mari was the queen bee, his effusive, fast-talking, popular sister. He was not exactly friends with her, but they honestly were not enemies, not with small generosities occasionally given, if never discussed. She glanced at him once but stayed in the center of focus with her posse, leading the argument about some new rule at school and a change in grading, certainly unfair and hurtful. She would have never diverted off point, probably, except two of her friends were looking at him, since girls will look.

"Hey, this is my brother, guys," Mari tossed off, "he's in a different school, don't ask, so that's why you think he's from outer space or something." With that she turned to another girl and dug into her sharply for a remark two sentences before the interruption. Two or three others threw in harsh opinions faster than ever, although the blistering pace of contention did not put the skids on carbohydrate-seeking – bagels and diet iced tea and low-fat yogurt.

He slid out of the way when Mari dove into the 'fridge. He picked up his mistreated cellphone and took possession of one corner of the kitchen, slugging a big gulp from the milk bottle occasionally. They all had long hair, he saw. Ponytails. He suspected volleyball. His glance went from one to the other in turn, like a scientist attempting to ascertain if this were all one species.

One of the girls, the least vocal, inched over near him.

"Mari should have at least said your name," she said softly. "I'm Kath."

He turned his eyes on her but did not change expression. He took another pull on the milk bottle.

Undeterred, she tried again. "What school?"

He held her gaze through a long pause. Then he gave it to her right between the eyes.

"Don't ever tell a guy, 'it's not you, it's me.' We know you're lying."

She reacted with one, two, three blinks, and a slow serious nod, and backed away carefully, but just as she turned to rejoin her sisters, said in a low voice, "Okay."

The others realized something happened by the look on their friend's face. Mari turned to confront him square, with all the intensity that one-hundred-and-two pounds might command.

"What did you say?"

Utter silence froze the kitchen. He stared her down. Hell, his sister was one of them. No exceptions. Just as she was about to open her mouth again, he raised his arms, still holding the neck of the milk bottle, scrunched his shoulders in a gesture of mock triumph and surrender, and unloaded loudly ...

"It's true, it's true, you people are correct, and

no shit Sherlock, all us guys want is sex."

He turned quickly and made a dramatic exit out the side door of the kitchen, hitting the stairs, stomping and clomping like the studliest of them all, milk in hand. He left behind a gaggle of bright laughing girls with the best possible ridiculous tale to tell.

this pleasure she indulged

Sunday morning, she awoke knowing what had happened in the night. She fell in love. Last night, dreamy and wistful. This morning, over the rainbow.

Can one fall in love in one's sleep?

She suspected so, because the irrepressible smiles this morning were the exposed bashful ones, smiles she would not wish her girlfriends to see, least not until enjoyed in private for a day. They kept spilling over into giggling fits. More amusing, the impeccable pun he made as they returned to their table after a waltz. She repeated it in her mind. Many times.

Oh, the wonderful wit and ways of him, a magical prince turning his intentions on her, over whom she must laugh and cry with blushing foolishness until she melted on the floor at his feet. Because she entertained such a fantasia – which two days ago would have made her nauseous – she knew she was in love.

Other signs could not be denied: everything seemed to radiate light from within, as if freshly made by God; she would not move fast, as if a foolish or precipitous action might bruise her bloom of happiness, tender and yearning as it was; the songs to which they danced last night played continuously in her mind, each one of them portentous and eternal, piercing with romance.

Also, she desired him with her carnal heart.

"Come give me that good-night kiss again," she said while standing in cotton pajamas at a mirror brushing her teeth. "Kiss me, I dare you."

She sensed her practical self, real as rain, standing immediately behind in an intimidating business jacket and pencil skirt, vigilant, concerned over this outbreak of foolish zeal for something made of air. That girl wanted to call a doctor.

Rejecting diminishment of her mood, she spun around in a huff.

"I won't see him until I cool off, okay?"

With a flip of the head, she turned her back on the stern femme in the suit.

There was her dress to put away. It lay over the back of a chair. Scattered around it, the accoutrements of ensemble: a light jacket she had worn over her shoulders; the glorious pumps from Tramps in which her toes had twirled all night; a jade and silver necklace with matching earrings; and the silken undergarments, beautiful, elegant, secretive.

She sat on the floor by the chair, caressing the folds of the dress, touching the other things one by one. The shoes, especially, were dear to her.

In the extremity of her condition, she daydreamed him removing all these things from her body, slowly making her naked from exactly these clothes. But then, stronger – pleasure in the fact that only she, only her female person, had known the intimacies under her dress. What keen pleasure savoring both dreams with the same emotion.

With a sigh, she stood and began gathering the garments. She fetched the crazy Tramps box and set the shoes inside. On impulse, she reached for a decorative barrette that had shaped her up-do and set it in the box, along with a tiny bouquet he had given her, so tasteful it hurt to look upon. As the box lid closed over her treasures, the doorbell rang.

She ran across the apartment, exuberant and dramatic as a dancer, sliding to a halt to look through the peephole. With a grand flourish, she yanked the door open, unconcerned about appearing in pajamas – *who cares in such a moment.*

It was flowers. She closed the door behind her, dropped the box on the floor, and held them in her arms. Scent expanded from the palest roses she had ever seen. Some red, some yellow, some lavender hid in the edges of them. Also, a delicate shade of blue. Yet these were harsh names for the reality. Each bloom played off the white roses also included, gently holding their hue, but barely, politely declining the offer to become hue-fulfilled themselves.

Surrounding the roses, greenery and twigs artfully arranged contrasted and complemented. It was breath-taking.

Her giggling returned now, the smiles that

turned to giggles. They accompanied her like
music while she arranged the flowers, naturally in
her best large crystal vase, naturally set in a place
of honor near her bed. She stared at them for
minutes. She rearranged twice, inhaling the subtle
tender scent. She thought of them as matching
her emotions, how they tugged at her, teased her.
This pleasure she indulged.

The note:

> For a moment, I worried these glorious flowers would be
> too much. But no, the opposite, if plain truth is the
> measure - they cannot say enough of my happiness in
> your company last night. You are magnificent. I hope
> they say it for me many times today, the beautiful roses
> and their scent.
> You are magnificent. - Josh.

See? See why you fall in love? More un-bashful-
bashful smiles with wet eyes. She danced around
the apartment opening windows on the fresh day,
singing the hit tunes from last night. She returned
to the flowers. She read the note again, slowly.

A cold wind swept across her back. She
stopped, note in hand, and took the stance of a
soldier, to fight a pitiless gust of danger stalking
her vulnerability.

*It's only hormones, it will fade like fog, we are
sensible and practical, do nothing absurd, life is
not a fairy tale* – a rude dispatch from pencil-
skirt-girl armed with a bullhorn, from somewhere
in the apartment.

The morning sun shone in her face. A faint

wisp of scent from the roses, or her love of them, wafted across. She sprang into action.

She checked to be sure her cellphone was fully charged. She decided to leave the dress thrown over the back of the chair, but straightened everything else in the apartment. In her dressing area, she chose a pair of athletic pants, a tee shirt, and everyday underwear and socks. Running shoes.

The pajamas went flying off. She stepped into a near-scalding shower, washing her hair, then standing still under the cascading water for minutes.

She confronted the practical girl, who now hovered obnoxiously close.

I won't text him or phone him for at least six hours while I consider the world's realities of romance in modern life with open eyes. I will find out why this cold wind is so bitchy. I will honor everything to be discovered before I take him in bed. I'll make him prove everything. I expect him to make me prove it all, too. He'd better, damn it.

"But I will have nothing less than roses," she said, water streaming down her naked body, smiling irrepressibly, as if freshly made by God.

had possibly existed

Here came their cool game at the train again. They stopped conversation at the subway entrance. Up through the grates in the sidewalk came the un-sound of no current arrivals or departures – they were between trains.

The two sharp teens held this to be double-edged news – no regret for a train they were now missing, but no assurance one was not just down the line, in which case they might still lose out. They tumbled down the entryway fast, through turnstiles fed access cards ready in hand. Hector had two flights to descend, Marta only one. This was a transfer station with two lines crossing, one above the other, deep in the Manhattan underground.

Then they heard the approaching sound of her local. Perfect timing, in position with probably half a minute to spare. He could tell no train was arriving on his platform one flight below, so he remained at the edge of hers. They naturally peered back up the tunnel and saw the headlights and the big red "F" on the front of the oncoming car. The rumble increased.

Marta resumed one piece of unfinished

business, a joke earlier interrupted by a stern study hall monitor with a mean look. She had to speak louder and louder as she neared the payoff – the F-train seemed determined to not slow up a bit until the very last second for braking.

Hector listened to the silly story. She might win today's competition. He would have to find something extremely dumb and cool for tomorrow – this girl was good. He kept nodding, she gesticulating wildly to get the story across.

This was the way of her, so dramatic. Last year, when sophomores, they made an oral presentation as biology lab partners. He pushed her to the front, sure her so-fresh teen face and bouncing hair would kick up the grade a letter or two. He was right. Or believed he was right. She gave him credit for the research privately, but not generously. He got her to agree to share the load more, next time. That was the beginning of them as an academic team.

The careening and rushing train came forth, its rudely unmitigated shriek of metal-on-metal preceding. Then, the braking noise. Marta's face, flushed and rushed, never showed doubt she would get the story in. The train slammed to a halt, followed by the loud mechanical crack of the doors opening, then that weird platform silence. Into it, with exquisite timing, Marta pounded home her punch line. They doubled up, laughing in fun. She danced backward into the train. Hector raised his eyes to his study buddy one more time, shaking his head.

He caught his breath. Her smile had vanished,

head rock-steady, holding his gaze with absolute intent. He knew his eyes had gone huge, that she saw it, that it did not alter her expression. She did not blink. Even the door closing did not change her aspect – her eyes remained locked on his through the glass in the door panel, until the train gathered itself for the two-hundredth time that day and pulled away down its track.

He did not move. No one else stood on the platform. After a moment, one of those forever moments, he realized he had resumed breathing. He took a step toward the down-flight of stairs which would probably take him to a train that might move him to the place he lived in a world that a few moments ago had possibly existed.

No one heard it, but Hector said it out loud there on the F-train platform.

"That was a kiss."

ribbons of satin

Dawn opened before him.
His poetic sensibility blossomed richly
through his patience, his quiet vigil on the
deck of the small house while elements of the
mountainside materialized as night failed. Pale
green appeared in the meadow, then a darker
shade of it in pines just beyond, to his left. In
hollows farther below, the dark seemed to cling
overlong, until, with the ascendance of the sun, he
understood – fog wallowing in the narrow
twisted ravine had been absorbing the new light.
Even this began to relent, for the sun was already
strong.

The fog melted back down the slope, torn by
lofty pines and oaks on the mountain's shoulders.
Should he maintain his watch, the final reward for
his eyes, he knew, would be the revelation of the
shining ocean beyond the last sharp ridge. The
clash of mountain and sea would be fought right
in front of him, if far below.

A rustling made him turn. A vision emerged
from the house, something no dawn had ever seen
– she who held his heart, in her first morning after

their first night.

"Lovely," she said of the dawn.

She wore a romantic morning gown, cream-colored linen across her shoulders and down to her waist, caught there by a satin sash of yet another shade of white, descending over the subtle rounding at her hips to trail beautifully down and behind in a shaped train on the floor. At her breast the garment wrapped modestly, allowing only a glimpse of the curving flesh beneath, the bodice crossed with ribbons of silk and satin, some tied, others provocatively loose. Against the pale skin of her neck and face, the subtly differentiated colors of the gown seemed more breathtaking for the barely darker contrast.

Yet, most sensual of all to the eye against this song of like white shades – a riveting cascade of black hair, straight, supple, and very long. It framed her face and fell over her shoulders, reaching to the waist in several places. Without ever seeming less than jet black, solid, yet in its shimmer when moving one believed variant hue lay hidden, perhaps colors never named, perhaps only visible to the vivid eyes of her lover in his poet's immoderation now.

"Lovely," he said.

"You've been awake ..."

"About an hour. I watched you sleeping. I imagined you'd sleep until noon."

She smiled at this delightful exaggeration. "That would be missing too much," she said, mischief in her voice.

Then delight deepened, became wells of

memory and emotion, until eyes spoke as eloquent as songs the power of the heart falling open. They wrapped each other in embrace, sweet, body to body, kissing.

"Oh God," she murmured, shaking. "Is that why they call it 'making love'? Because you need more love each day to stand how good it is?"

"It must be."

"I need quite a bit of love right now. It took me ten minutes to put on this gown." She moved back to let him take her in from head to bare toes, which arched out past the hem of the dress.

"You are swimming in cream."

She nodded, smiling. With each movement of her head the splendid black tresses shifted and settled. "Perhaps ... perhaps that's my mission today. To see if I can survive a shock like this."

"How can I help?" he asked.

She looked at him silently, adoring. He absorbed her deep gaze, vowing to not miss any like this, ever.

"I'm might kiss you until you faint," he offered.

She laughed and brought her hand to cover her mouth. He stepped close.

"Undo these ribbons and kiss your breasts until you swoon."

"This isn't helping."

"And caress the side of your hip, all the way down to your knees."

"Stop."

"Or ... or ... worship you from afar, fragile as you are. Keep my adoration remote, no passionate glances, withhold whispers that should have been placed in your ear. Until you can love without fainting."

He had spoken with no irony.

"I never believed anyone would talk to me like this. For real. Like a love letter from another century, read out loud."

"It's too late now. You've made your bed with the wild poet."

"Shouldn't you say, 'now you've got to sleep in it'?"

"Even the sleeping was erotic, don't you think?"

"Yes! Were we touching?"

"Probably. I know one thing – the scent of that bed went into our dreams."

This comment, clearly, reached deep into her vulnerable center – she went speechless, having absorbed it unprotected. Her eyes glistened.

Make me talk like this by your beauty, my words arousing you, the glorious morning on this mountainside arousing you, the memory of your body taking mine inside arousing you. Else why am I a poet?

He lifted her in his arms and carried her into the mountainside house, the long tresses of silken black hair and ribbons of satin trailing behind, lifted by the gentlest breath of air rising from the sea below.

impossibly vibrant

Pancakes.

Dressed in pajamas, the sun barely risen, she brazenly concocted morning-after breakfast, betting the outré scene with its overstated obvious would be answered with an in-the-know smile. She was confident of such an outcome – he was that ironic.

So, pecans. Butter softening. Maple syrup, a bottle sitting in a blue saucepan at the simmer. Freshly brewed coffee – of course. In a bowl, flour, sugar, salt, eggs, buttermilk, and a big wooden spoon to stir it all. She sardonically wished for his appearance the instant she held the bowl in the crook of her arm, beating in strong strokes, making pancake batter. Would that picture crack him up or what?

The windows of the breakfast nook stood open, invoking morning coolness redolent with earth and dew. She set her table there. The glasses and silver, immaculate, glinted in the low angles of the sun. A bowl of red berries, pure cream in a glass bottle, two crisp napkins – these showed off colors of preternatural brilliance. Likewise, a carafe of orange juice set in a pitcher of ice – impossibly vibrant. She arranged pansies in a bud vase, admiring for a lingering second. How keen, the color, so exultant the soft shape of velvety flower petals glowing chartreuse, magenta, pale violet.

"How fine, the world," she whispered, a shimmer in her eyes.

"What's this?"

She spun around. She spread arms wide to invoke the elaborate mise-en-scène. "Ta-da."

A king sheet enfolded his frame, the million-thread-count Egyptian cotton masterpiece from her bed. Stubble covering chin, black hair sticking up all crazy, the soft puff of sleep showing in his eyes – but they glowed.

"This is very ambitious," he said.

"You need breakfast."

"Smells good. Coffee smells good." He shuffled deeper into the kitchen, the cotton extravaganza trailing behind. "Whoa," he said as he got closer, "you're actually making pancakes?"

"What's wrong with that?"

"What are we, four?"

"You're supposed to be amused." She pouted. "It's cute."

He got in her way on purpose. "I want a lot of them."

"Yeah?"

"A tall stack."

"I can do that."

He opened his arms. "Come in here."

She twined arms around his neck and pulled him close. He was naked and smelled good. He draped the sheet around, creating a tent. They pressed against each other, fitting in place, recalling how their embraces went. His lips moved under her chin, over her jaw line, now finding her mouth, unleashing their oral joy, making her whimper.

"This means you like me," she said when his mouth lifted off to re-aim.

"I like this, and this," he whispered as he placed kisses one by one, "and to the side like this, and like this, and this." He moved down her throat with the obvious intention of liking inside her pajama top. "I like you here, and here, and here." He tried with lips to unfasten the topmost button.

"Food first."

She pushed him away playfully and spun around to attend to the makings. More beating with the spoon. Fetching a plate for butter. A drop of water on the skillet to assure it was hot enough. *These will be the best damn pancakes he ever ate* – she was fierce about that.

Then she realized he had not moved, was standing right behind her. She turned slowly.

This was her cool boyfriend, unshaven, tousled, covered by a huge ivory sheet like a Tantric ritual gown, shaking his head. She reached back and turned off the burner under the cast iron skillet. "What?" He stared back, comically dismal. "What?"

"I love you."

She shook. He had never said it. She never said it – only hedged like Jane Austen in 1811, '*I greatly esteem him*,' but with a glorious romp of twenty-first century sex on top. She bubbled over.

"Boy, you are in trouble."

He nodded, helpless.

She spun completely around three-sixty like a crazed ballerina, laughing, then threw her arms around him again.

"You stay over, you show up for breakfast, and now you throw the L-word, oh, this is serious trouble," she prodded, sardonic and theatrical.

"You don't have to take such advantage of it."

"Oh, yes I do. I'll play it for all its worth. Man, these pancakes are going to taste so damn good now."

"Stop."

"I wish I had the 'I love you' on video."

He groaned. "Oh my God, what the hell did I just do?" He sat down with a thud. The irony she'd hoped for sparkled in his eyes. "I'm a goner."

"Wanna take it back?"

"I can't."

"I'll let you."

"I can't."

"We're good at ignoring."

"You're not going to say it?"

"No."

"Good," he said. "At least one of us is keeping the lid on it. What a disaster."

"That's right. Sex and fun and dates and fun and sex. And that's all. I'm in charge of that."

"Come on, say it," he said.

"No."

"Say it."

"No."

She let out a full-throated whoop and spun back to her work with much clatter and shuffle. Sizzle and steam rose above the stove. She glanced through misty eyes at the windowsill where a second small vase of blooms flaunted their outrageous colors. Impossibly vibrant.

Suddenly, she froze, held her breath, and tightened her armor. Not all the way, so small thrills and play could still get in.

Now things happened quickly. Coffee at the table. She poured juice from the iced pitcher. With one or two more swirling exhibitions, she set down a beautiful stack of high-risen steaming cakes, perfectly golden brown. Hers were ready too. She sat across, smiling wide.

"Try 'em."

He cut a wedge with a fork. As he took hold of the maple syrup, she reached over the table with a knife holding butter and deposited a generous dollop. She watched, fascinated, as he ate the first bite. His eyes grew large.

"Oh, my, my. That is really good," he exhorted, smacking his lips, not in parody. "Lordy, that's good."

She began eating with lusty enthusiasm. They annihilated the pancakes and joked in delight of the whole scene. He still wore the beautiful sheet around his shoulders. The food was delectable, the redolence of pecans and maple ridiculous.

She stopped. He didn't notice. She blinked three times. She leaned across the table. "Say it again."

He put his fork on his plate and stared her

down. "Now *you* are in trouble," he said.

She nodded. In his pause, she opened her heart for it.

"I love you," he said.

"You do?"

"I love you."

She stared into his beautiful face. "That went in like an arrow."

"Don't say it back. Just let it wound you good."

a woman alive on the earth

While two fine friends lived in town with whom daily contact would be delightful, Tibi established with them the expectation and acceptance of solitude for herself in the hilltop house three months every year. It was the time in late winter her man was away at sea. The friends let Tibi come down to them at will, and only ventured up the hill at the back of town when purpose-asked, for dinner, laughing, and singing. Otherwise, they left Tibi alone for as long as she wanted. They knew she was weaving fine cloth for new clothes, knew the year was always thought to start in that small house when the couple reunited each April and put on their spring raiment. This had been so for eleven years.

This year, a long passage of time without a visit in either direction fell in March. There was no concern, however. Occasionally, the high free voice in song from the house above floated dimly over the streets – they knew she was happy.

Then, a special invitation arrived. They were requested for a feast, just the two of them, without children or husbands. The invitations arrived folded inside squares of beautiful new-woven linen, dyed bright and colorful, delivered by the student of one of the two ladies, a boy who lived near Tibi. On the appointed day, the friends walked arm in arm joyfully up the hill in late afternoon.

They were greeted with every warmth and pleasure of reuniting, more so than usual, in fact. Tibi fairly shone to receive them. First looks after the few weeks apart seemed especially keen, and the laughing and talking and eating commenced at once. The house was fastidiously clean, but wonderfully strewn with evidence of weaving and sewing all about. Because of fair weather, many windows stood open into evening. At dusk Tibi lit candles. Voices became more subdued, and a few choice secrets flew from mouth to mouth, not quite gossip, but quite as fascinating.

Then Tibi got their attention because she stopped talking – she said nothing for quite a while. They noticed. They saw also a new expression on the loved face, as if far along in the deliciousness of something the others had not yet tasted. They began to ask her to reveal her inner secret. Tibi stood up at the big window at the front of the house. She looked out to sea.

"I have enjoyed my loneliness again. I treasured it this time like no other. He will return soon, and yes, that is always the beginning of sharing and belonging. Of being wife. I welcome it every year." She was quiet for a moment or two, looking out. Then she slowly walked to the table and looked into the eyes of her friends, they who knew her well.

"But this is the end of my sojourn alone each

winter as before. Not again. Not for many many years."

They urged her to continue. How could this be?

"As last year ended, my Arjani and I fell into so deep a place of marriage, I felt as if what went before were only a pretty little kiss. No. This was a fire, and like entering a palace, and like ... like heaven."

They waited, fascinated, for her to continue.

"Why did God give this? I did nothing and Arjani did nothing, but there was no time in all our life as that time. We mated so many times."

Tibi was not embarrassed to say this to her dear ones. It was natural. But suddenly their faces changed. They knew what came next as it came.

"We thought my time had passed, that my time was never to be. But not so, you see."

They were already crying tears of joy for their friend, crying for the vanquishing of sad times before.

"I am with child. He does not know. It will be born early in fall. I am happy to be a woman alive on the earth."

shades of green unfolded

Ten years after he was left alone in the world, Martin departed from his ways in the north fields.

It started with the nitrogen. His hand went reaching for the sacks piled as usual in the corner of a shed, destined to be spread on 371 acres, the stuff the big AG people from UMN insisted winter wheat could not live without. If asked the moment before, he would have surely replied 'steady's she goes,' as with the last thirty-six years. This time, as he reached for it, when the N-30-P-4 provided its familiar scent, he stopped.

"At donn smell raht."

Without another word, he closed the shed door.

At harvest, his yield was down 24%, but he did not flinch. He planted nitrogen-fixing peas and tilled them back into the soil next cycle. This green fertilizer got some of the shortfall back. Things stayed steady like that for two more years in the fields.

Then, in the first afternoon of the next harvest, he abruptly let out the clutch of the combine a hundred and fifty yards into the field off the southwest corner. He turned the machine off. For a time, he wandered slowly in the tall wheat, making erratic circles around the silent giant harvester. He stood still for fifteen minutes with face to the lowering sun, looking back to the farmhouse, with a fluffing wind moving his hair. Then, with no change of expression, he climbed back on the rattling ravenous contraption and took in his crop.

Three weeks later, at the end of August, two cars approached on the perimeter road and raced down his drive. Five boys piled out. They wore high school football jackets. Martin grinned inside – *could there be that many young bucks around anymore*. He was sure two were linebackers. He squared up against one of them, who smiled broadly.

"Okay, Mr. Johnson, you wanted a gang and I've got you a gang."

"Ah didn't say right out a gang did ah, James?"

"Oh, yes sir, you did. Now don't deny it."

"Ya telling me true they ain't smashin up ther thumbs soonze ah pass the hammas round?"

James, who was in construction with his dad, laughed. The boys said their names quickly.

"Well it's sure to blaze up real quick taday, so let's see what ah got ya into. Jus watch fa lemnaid baht noon an a big wad a tweny dollah bills ta pass round bah the end a day."

Several gang members' eyes got big listening to this drawl. James had warned them to not smirk out loud on pain of big smack. As they rambled down the lane along the wheat field, James dropped back and whispered to them.

"It's from the south."

"Where the hell in the south for God's sake."

"Way south. He just never switched over to regular Minnesota. So, shut up."

"There he is again, I told you."

"Where?"

"That's his truck right across the way, just pulled in."

"Well really, look at that, I guess you might be right, Bebee. Three times this week, really?"

"Three times right at this time, right about when everyone's gone back to work. This can't be no never-mind, just like I said."

The two friends were in agreement that the seldom-seen Martin was coming to town late in fall for lunch. Frequently. They watched him enter the café across from a vantage point in their gift shop. They chattered away for a few minutes over this unusual disturbance in the town's alignments. Then there was a pause. Bebee smiled at her friend.

"You stay here, I'm going over there for an egg-salad sandwich," she told the other.

"He's smarter than you think, now."

"Never mind, I don't care if he figures out I'm spying, because I am," said Bebee as she breezed out into the street.

As usual, only an occasional table remained occupied as Martin crossed to his spot. It was a booth at the back, adjacent the kitchen. Within moments, that which could be counted on as inevitable occurred – the arrival at the table of Emma.

"Martin," she said.

"Ah wanted at chicken pot pah agin, but ya probably wrote it down already," he said with a wry smile.

Emma faced him with hand on hip. "Now a good waitress won't ever write it up like that, even when a regular walks in at his regular time and sits at his regular table, and that's a fact."

"Ahm a regaler?" he asked with a downturn of his smile.

"Now that's a term of goodness, Martin, so no getting sour on it."

"Ah hope ya don't say waitress agin."

"Just my little joke."

Emma owned the diner.

"Well, kindly tell the waitress ta tell the cook ta put one a them pahs in for me right soon, mamm, an can she bring over mah coffee, too."

She turned and walked away with a scrunch of her forehead.

"Ah hope ya don't say mamm again," she tossed over her shoulder in perfect mockery of his drawl.

Just as the last of the other lunch patrons headed to the door, it opened to admit Bebee striding in, seeming all business.

"Why, hello Martin," she said seeming surprised. "We hardly ever see you in town anymore."

"Hello, Miss Bebee," he said carefully, seeming

unsurprised.

"Now I know you can cook some on your own, but you must have fallen under the spell of Emma's food, and who can blame you. I myself had a brown bag, but I put it aside, just had to come over here for something anyway, don't you know?"

He was saved from further interaction when Emma emerged from the back, and after setting down his coffee, engaged her customer in the sandwich transaction, to go. Nevertheless, there were pleasantries all around, a few comments with portentous intent, and a meaningful glance at Emma and over to Martin before she was ushered out. Emma watched her bustle across the street. She turned to walk to the back of the diner shaking her head in mock disgust.

"They're spying on us from the Busy Bee gift shop, Martin."

"Ain't that priddy close ta busybody?" he remarked.

Emma laughed.

The town, evidently, was left no alternative to accepting the new arrangement through the arduous Minnesota winter – Martin was calling on Emma. Afternoons, they had the place mostly to themselves, and Emma's preparations to set up the dinner rush for her new night cook proved easy. His booth became their booth three days a week. Sometimes they chatted about the snow and the partially grown wheat that lay dormant beneath it for miles in every direction around the town. He always seemed un-bored hearing about doings in the restaurant each visit.

They liked playing cards – Gin Rummy. Also, a game of reading out to each other from the St. Paul Pioneer Press the dubious goings-on in Los Angeles and New York City and the like, places that must have been made up like a silly joke, they pretended. "Let's not go there," they said.

Emma drew him into her love of crossword puzzles. They worked them out together, clue by clue. Every once in a while, Emma began to pencil in an answer, but by spelling it verbatim as he pronounced it, failed laughingly to facilitate it fitting the space. Martin always gave an amused stone stare back to this type of flirting.

And sometimes, since each possessed decades, there was reminiscence, unfolding, small turns of the heart.

Eventually, the cold receded. Enough warmer days passed for the wheat to become convinced it was no false alarm – it resumed life and spurted ahead. Everyone was willing to endure mud for a stretch, in payment for mild days, gentle wind, and general renewal.

Spring in Minnesota.

One Monday, Martin rolled up to the diner in mid-afternoon. He had never come on Monday before. Emma looked at him in surprise. There was no one else in the front of the house.

"Martin."

"I remember yor words from last week Emma, 'bout young Alex easin' into Monday afternoons for you, ta take the reins, rhat?

"Yes," she said. "He's here in the back now."

"Can ya leave off?"

There was a moment when the awkwardness of this out-of-place request strained, then eased. She accepted. Then she more than accepted.

"Yes."

"Emma, I want ya to walk mah farm."

She held his glance steady for a perfect quiet moment. "I'm changing shoes, then. Just give me a few minutes. Do you want coffee?"

"No, thanks."

They drove north out of town with an occasional word between them. He announced he had "g'loshes" in the trunk for her. There was a shared belief that this was spring at last, hence one could walk out into the world again, even if wet.

When they turned off the county road, Emma slid forward in her seat. It was straight in, directly west, to the center of the farm, with the fields of young wheat shimmering green on their right. Martin brought them to a stop along the drive where a side lane branched to the north twenty yards from the farmhouse. He walked around to fetch Emma out into the wonderful air.

"Oh Martin, that's a beautiful old house," she said, looking across at it. "Just like I pictured it from your telling."

"Ah got me a little plan, though. Just a little walk down this here lane fust, not up no mountains at all."

While the wheat fields to the north and east stretched generally flat, with a few rolling swells, to the west lay a serious woodlot, thick with mature trees, but orderly at their feet from the clearing of brush. The wood clung to a disturbed landscape, first down into a divide, then up two or three modest rises to ridge tops. The north lane they intended to walk formed the demarcation between the cultivated and the wild.

Emma put her arm through his.

"Show me," she said, smiling.

The sun had only three hours left in its day, yet still hung above one of the ridges. It sent slanting yellow light through the woods, unimpeded by any leaves, since they were all on the ground. The shadows of tall birch and hemlock trunks crossed their path at an angle. Gradually, the lane curved to the west slightly and descended gently, but the wheat field clung tight on their right. With a slight breeze and the slanting rays, multitudinous shades of green unfolded, flowing through the waving strands.

"It's really grass," Emma said.

"Yes, it is. Grass we let go to the very end, it turns gold 'n brown, and then we git the seed. I'm jus a farma who watches the grass grow." He laughed.

"I hear water," she said, turning her head to the left.

"You'll see it, round th' nex bend."

The lane made a serious left turn and descended, leaving the wheat behind. Revealed on the slope to the southwest, a grove with trees of magnificent girth, all of a kind, hundreds of them, obviously cared for – there were no weed trees or underbrush at all. At the foot of the hill lay a long wooden shed with chimneys. Every tree on the hillside was naked of leaves, and the effect was dramatic, like a stock-still legion occupying the high ground.

"What is this?" she asked, stopping and pointing.

"Well, that's mah sugar bush. Seven acres a Sugar Maples."

"Oh."

"I ain't made the sugar in twelve years, though. I keep them nice even so. Before that, I got plenty a gallons for thirty-fi years. Ah make good sugar."

"I just bet."

"When the fust frost gits here in September, standing rhat here, the sight a that whole hill, the color ..." He left off, shaking his head.

"And you don't have to rake a bit when they all fall off."

They chatted and laughed about that as they came to the end of the westwarding portion of the lane – it turned right and north again, for reason. It was banked up now and reinforced against the spring onrush of a strong south-flowing stream, which must come down from the farther ridges north and west.

"It don't run this strong all year, you can bet," Martin told her. "But it gets rambunctious now."

She turned to face him.

"So beautiful here, Martin. This is where you have lived your life. In beauty all the time."

"I was mostly more worried 'bout the cost a sprayin' and mortgages and the laik."

"Yes, I know."

"Ah want to go a few hundred yards more, Emma, up the lane. Right up there." He pointed to the right and above, where it was obvious some new work had been done on the road and surrounding land to make a new place.

As they ascended, she pointed upstream, and commented on a bridge across the water and a path winding up west and away over the far ridge. He didn't respond.

They climbed. The lane wound across the face of the hill until it finally ended in a flat. It was obvious this was a power place. The stream flowed fast, one-hundred feet below. The hardwood forest clinging to the valley running south glowed with the faintest green haze, for some trees were of a kind that allowed eager early buds. Looking back over their shoulder they could catch a swatch of the vibrant green wheat field, since they had climbed back up nearly level with it. There was not the slightest hint of county road, other farms, or anything left behind in the world.

"I'm sixty-seven years now, Emma, but ahm going to build here. Fresh."

"It takes my breath away."

"Ah got one more thing. Come on."

He led her by the hand across the flat space sure to take the foundation and pad for a house. They entered a small jut-out of heavy trees, butternut and birch. He took her down a path going through. Emerging from the wooded path, she threw her hand to her mouth with an exclamation. She ran forward.

Martin had built a covered pavilion at the edge of the woods in the side of the hill. Stepping in and spinning around, she did not ask where the oak and maple woods of the beams, lattice and balustrade came from – it was a silly question. But the floor, twenty feet across in octagon shape, was something other: solid-piece 14-inch squares that varied in color from deep reddish-brown heartwood to creamy white from the sapwood, repeated over and over, with grain brought out skillfully.

Emma ran across the pavilion to take in the view, which resulted in a squeal of delight. She touched the wood with evident joy. She had thrown off her muddy galoshes before running in, and now threw off her shoes, too.

"What is this floor?"

"That's mah special wood, from two tamarack trees ahve been watchin' since ... since long ago. It was their tahm, they were dyin'. To git it to look lahk at, well you gotta have a big tree an' slice at a certain angle."

"You dreamed this place up, Martin," she said twirling around a little and glancing at him with excitement. He moved slowly near her, but silently. "Only a man young at heart would do this, you know. And never a word all winter long. How could you not tell me?"

"Ah was takin you in."

"But you must have done the work last fall, most of it."

"Yes. Last summa. I had a bunch a roustabouts

hammerin' away."

"Before you came courting to the café?"

"Emma, ah knew about you well before, you just have no recollection."

"When did you see me?"

"You know how you usually go walkin' in town every day 'tween lunch and dinner."

"Yes. To go home for a spell."

"I spotted you one day, and then, by God, I just had this and that takin' me inta town right bout the raht time and somehow I ended up parkin', listen to music and watchin' out from where you couldn't see me, now and then. En one day I had your daughter, ah new she was your daughter, outside the grange ..."

"She's always over there."

"... and she kindly sat with me, talkin'. She let me ask about you. I didn't ask too much."

"I can't believe this."

"Ya know what that smart gal asked me at the end, I know ... I was I guess pretty easy to figure ... she said, 'Cain I tell my mom your askin, or are you setting your cap for her and I should just watch?' She lahks me, I think."

"Amazing. She never said a thing."

"An so this is mah way. You can see I'm going to ask you now."

"Yes."

"Ah didn't build the house first 'case someone besides me might want it certain ways."

"I see."

"You can bet that winding lane going back down past the stream gets snowed under. So, behind here's a little road 'at takes a straight line easy back to the county road. We can get out any tahm, 'cause I'll just push the snow away on the flat."

"Yes." Emma's eyes held steady and shone with pride and excitement. Magic light from the lowering sun on the beautiful wood of the pavilion glowed all around them.

"An 'at bridge to the north?" He pointed down to it.

"Yes?"

"This I must tell you 'bout. Over the bridge and up the path takes you on that ridge across the way." They looked out across the valley. "The woods keep goin' for a couple miles 'cause they join up with other farms. But right at the edge of mah acres there's a clearin'. I have to walk up there on times, Emma. There's a grave there."

She sobered but did not turn out the light in her eyes. She just nodded and waited for two long breaths. Then she gently placed her hand on his chest, only the simplest of touches.

"Ah told her 'bout you this mornin'."

Emma waited.

"Will you put your life with mahn?"

"Yes."

"Can you live here above this valley?"

"Yes."

"You might keep the café right on goin' or you might not. Either way."

"Yes."

"I'll never forget our winter in there. That's when you grew warm in me, Emma. I came to love you. Hope that ain't too silly comin' from an old farma."

She didn't say her love back, just held it in her eyes with tears falling. Martin took his bride in his arms and kissed her well.

eyes full of light and laughter

Mariko took a new lover.

It started in January at the Moscone Center, of all places, during a convention for graphics professionals and techs. The swirling mix of strangers, and her situation of being a designer yet having no imperative at the show, contributed. Mostly, she was susceptible – her last big thing lay far behind, and her heart ached for romance.

She caught a glimpse of him at the tail end of a software demonstration to which he brought a confident, well-articulated speaking style and alert intelligence. Apparently, he had bolted out of the demo area quickly after his performance, because she loitered on its fringes, hoping to catch more of him, to no avail.

She set her intention on him the next day. She entangled him in a complex discussion between demos, with subtle flirting engaged. She accelerated when his focus both widened beyond show-context but also sharpened inward as each nugget of her femme intrigue dropped into the vortex.

Mariko was not a fool. Regardless of her

ripeness, she was hardly open to someone living far away, or anyone toxic. The object of her attention called the Mission District his home, had for over ten years. What else did she discover? He was thirty-one years old, liked dogs, films from the 1950s, and obscure brands of scotch whiskey. He found sailing – the kind with sails – deeply pleasurable; they would be out on San Francisco Bay together once spring arrived, that was inevitable.

There had been two big loves. She was immediately on guard over the last one, a girl who left him to live in the East and not be married. Her jealousy came from suspicion of that girl's talent in bed.

How much time was required to amass these tidbits? That first night over drinks, the next night at a dark performance coffeehouse, and substantially during a date in Sausalito the following weekend that included superb seafood, wine from Calistoga, and two ferry rides across San Francisco Bay.

Mariko would always carry a treasure – the motion of her heart from his insistence to know her intention about children. Yes, wanted them, she assured him. Yes, more than one. Yes, keen to nurture when young as her primary concern. He marked her soul by the directness of his intent, how he would not look away from her eyes while asking, how he never pretended his questions were idle curiosity, how he would not rest until her gentle smiles and one or two repeats put the issue of sincerity beyond question. Finally, in a coup de main, she provided what must have been stunning to his ears – she called herself a smart, sexy mom waiting for the children to arrive.

Funny. Having declared her availability and eagerness for such a role, she now craved him like a girlfriend does, wanted a passionate love affair madly. Within two weeks, Mariko's ardent kissing and eyes full of light and laughter brought him to her bed. Right from the start, it was spectacular.

"What time is it?"

"Two fifteen."

"We're spending Saturday afternoon in bed, aren't we?"

"I'm only getting out to pee and get oranges."

"What about to get another condom?"

A dramatic pause. They looked at each other inquisitively.

"Let's stop using them."

"You must be out of your mind."

"Really. Don't you want to feel us rubbing? Not rubber. Rubbing!"

"Very funny."

They paused to split a big, ripe, outrageously delicious orange, delighted with how much juice it contained. It was so sweet they could not finish it. It became clear the topic remained on the bed.

"How long do you think we should be together before even considering a kid?"

"Wait a minute. That's scary, the way you put it. We have four months now, but we have to be forever first."

"Forever?"

"Before we get pregnant one of us has to say 'forever' and then the other has to say 'forever' and then the first one has to say 'forever' again and then you kiss and then you have a big party where everyone dances and gets drunk and all the young boys fall in love with the bride."

"You say it first."

"No, you."

"I want to know we're forever for a while, but not say it yet, but not pretend we aren't, but not get married."

"Is that like having your wedding cake and eating it too?"

"I'd call it tasting it, seeing how scrumptious it is."

"Seeing how long it'll last?"

That stopped them. They sat close, face to face, amid the chaotic sheets and pillows. The taste of the orange and the smell of its oils on their hands resounded like a fine melody behind it all.

"Are you nervous?"

"No."

"We both want children."

"I do."

"So do I."

"Fourteen or fifteen?"

"Just a few. A perfect few."

They were practically whispering now. Mariko thrilled to the existential nakedness of it, eyes wide with aliveness. They inched closer.

"Here goes. I needed to have sex with you first. To be lovers for a time. To see if you had a drive. And yes, if it would last. Also, to see if when we fall out of love we have the guts to get it back on fire. Is that too pragmatic?"

"We fell out and got back."

"Yes. Twice in four months."

"Do I have a drive?"

"You would do it again right now, right?"

"Yes."

"Right now, you're turned on and ready to make love again, right now?"

"Yes."

"This is your drive as I have come to know it."

They laughed silly over the joke, rolling around in the sheets, naked to naked, 'simmering the kundalini,' as he liked to say.

"I'll drive you if you drive me."

"Drive me, oh please drive me."

Gradually, the affection in touch gentled them, while the question waited to come around again. They lay utterly still in each other's arms, face to face. Mariko had never felt closer to another human being in her life. Never. It truly seemed two people, one soul.

"I'm not going to have a marriage without sex."

"Me neither."

"Before, during, or after children."

"Me neither."

"But there's a price to pay for this love affair. I think you know what I'm saying."

"I think so."

"The sex is so good. Marriage is scary. We could get stuck, not get married, because we're afraid to lose the pleasure. Afraid it would ruin sex."

"What would be the worst?"

"Getting tempted to say, 'Let's not tempt fate. Let's just keep going like this and not risk getting married'."

"Would we still have children?"

"That's just it. If we're afraid to get married, either we won't have children, which would be a tragedy, or we'd have them, but without the sea change from marriage vows, not a good thing in a family to be missing, or you know, we'd probably end up making a baby by accident."

"Sheesh."

Then their simple little Saturday became a day of eternity.

"We both know the sex will be good. We're driven."

"Yes."

"Here's how we find out if we have the courage to get married. We take away the sex and begin courting for the grand prize."

"Oh my God. Do we have to go that far? It's insane, we're so happy, why would we ever stop? You're scaring me."

"If we can't get engaged right here, right now, naked in this bed, I think we should stop having sex."

If granted lovers the courage to look fate in the eye, fear-challenged and exultant, so it was, then, in the bed of Mariko and the man whose heart she had won.

~~~~~

The dancing had begun. Everyone was so happy, the dance floor filled at once.

At a table off in a corner sat a lone occupant, a young gentleman eight years of age, sharp as anything in a suit of fine wool, with a silk tie his father picked out.

He was quiet. He was not fazed by the tumult all around. He had eyes for one person only, the slender, sweet, Asian-looking woman in the white satin gown, swirling across the floor in the arms of, well, not in his arms was all he knew. She was beautiful.

Then, above the babble and music, the voice of the girl reached across the room to fall on him, her laughter so rich and free it broke open his young heart.

He could not bear to look for a moment. His gaze fell to the table and that which lay centered on the ivory tablecloth, radiant in the afternoon sun – a silver bowl full of large, magnificent oranges.

by john caedan

Stories
eyes full of light and laughter

Novels
the preludes
the white sky

Coming-of-Age
SaraIRL.com

johncaedan.com

about this edition

Images:
model, composition, and render
by John Caedan

Text font:
EB Garamond
Designed by Georg Duffner, Octavio Pardo
for Google Fonts

Titles font
Allison
Designed by Robert Leuschke
For Google Fonts

Text block style:
Ragged right justification, non-hyphenated.
While writers are strictly advised to format their
texts with equal length lines,
I inquired if that were true for poetry.
No.